THE ADVENTURES OF

AND THE OCEAN MONSTER

By Jade Harley

The Adventures Of Lola and the Ocean Monster

First published in 2017 www.theadventuresoflola.com ISBN 978-1977885524

Copyright © Jade Harley 2017 Cover art © Craig Phillips

This is a work of fiction. Names, characters, locations, themes and incidents are either products of the author's imagination or used in a fictitious manner. Any resemblance to actual persons, living or dead, or actual events is purely coincidental.

This book is dedicated to Liam and Lana.

Live simply.
Dream big.
Be grateful.
Give love.
Laugh lots.

CONTENTS

ONE

SURF'S UP

Well, hello my friends! It's been so long since we last spoke and so much has happened that I hardly know where to begin. Perhaps a quick recap of my adventures is in order, especially for any new readers joining us.

Spoiler alert!!

If you don't want me to ruin the surprise then please stop reading immediately, read my first book and come back to this one later - you don't want to miss out on all the fun now do you?

You're still with me, okay let's get down to business.

I'm LOLA and I'm a fairy, not a regular fairy mind you, I like to think I've got a certain style all of my own.

I've got blue hair and big boots, I love running and jumping and kicking things, I'm a wicked kickboxer and when I grow up I want to be a world famous adventurer, exploring the farthest corners of the earth and protecting creatures great and small.

My best friends are Allie and Jet – they are honestly the greatest friends a girl could have and we pretty much spend all our time together.

I used to live in the Blue Mountains but now I live in Byron Bay with the Water Fairies in an awesome cave by the ocean.

I have a pretty wild imagination that can get me into trouble sometimes but last year my imagination led me on an adventure. You see one day at school I overheard my Headmaster talking about a potential disaster with a new mysterious teacher called Mr. Holt and I was determined to get to the bottom of it. My investigation unearthed a conspiracy that led all the way back to the King and I had to flee my hometown in order to solve it. My journey took me to Byron Bay where I met the Queen of the Water Fairies, Katia, who took me under her wing. I learned I had magical powers far beyond my imagination (the King had kept most of our powers secret from us) and with an army of Water Fairies by my side I returned to my hometown to save the day.

And that's where I left you...at the party to end all parties!
You see after we showed our mean King a thing or two, we had
a party in the ruins of our town.

The King was utterly defeated and became a hermit - he
still lives in the Palace ruins with a few faithful servants and
the Queen. Their daughter, the Princess, left the very next day
with one of the brave Water Fairies that fought alongside us in
battle. I've been told it's true love, so good for her.

The rest of the town went searching for new places to call
home. A few settled in other parts of the Blue Mountains. After
all, it IS one of the most beautiful places on earth. But the
majority of the townsfolk were inspired by the events of the
summer and decided to look for a new adventure further afield.
Some fairies settled in Brisbane on the coast and others I
heard headed to Melbourne and even as far as Perth.

What about my best friends in the whole world, Jet and
Allie? I hear you ask.

Well, thankfully we all moved to the same place and I still
see Jet and Allie every day.

That's where this story begins...

Mum and Dad didn't put up much of a fight when I
suggested that we all move to Byron Bay and live with the
Water Fairies. In fact, I think they were quite relieved that we
had somewhere to go. I was grounded for months and I couldn't
really blame them. After all, I did scare them half to death by
running away. It was only right that they punish me, but I'd
been on my best behaviour ever since we'd arrived in Byron
Bay, and I hoped that they had noticed. I had a HUGE
opportunity awaiting me, but it meant me going away again,
and I REALLY hoped I'd earned enough brownie points to get
their permission. You see last year we found out about a
training camp for Protector Fairies, it turned out that Mr. Holt
was only pretending to be a teacher at our school and was in
fact a Protector Fairy! (Protector Fairies are the coolest fairies
on the planet and it is my dream to be one when I grow up.)
Both he and Katia have been on missions all over the world,

9

saving endangered species, protecting the environment and fighting for the rights of all creatures – now I had the chance to go to the same training academy that they had graduated from and to say that I wanted to go was an understatement!

One morning as we sat silently basking in the morning sun, I couldn't bear to wait any longer. I let Mum and Dad finish their juices before I nervously raised the topic.

"Mum, Dad...you know how last Summer I disappeared without telling you, and you were so cross, but it was all okay in the end?..." I quickly rushed out the words, hoping not to remind them how differently things could have ended.

"Well, I wouldn't put it quite like that, but yes I certainly remember," replied Mum stiffly.

"So there's a training camp for Protector Fairies that starts next week and I've been invited to join, which is a huge honour. I really want to go, can I please?" I begged.

"I don't know LOLA, is it dangerous?"

I sighed; I swear my Mum still thinks I'm like five or something.

"Mum, it teaches you how to protect others, so we are the ones keeping everyone safe. I'm pretty brave you know Mum, and now that I have so many wicked new powers I'm sure I'll be even braver! You know it's my dream to become a Protector Fairy. Please say I can go," I pleaded.

"Let your father and I discuss it. Is there a leaflet or something? How can I consider this seriously when I know nothing about it?" questioned my Mum.

"Jet's parents already said yes," I added, hoping that would help persuade her.

"Well that's good for Jet then isn't it, but Jet is a year older than you. You're still only thirteen, LOLA. I know you think that you're all grown up, but you're still a child and we're still your parents. I want to know more about it. How long would you stay there? Is this instead of school, and if so, what about your regular lessons? Do you still take those? I have lots of questions, LOLA...is there a teacher or someone else who we can meet with to learn more about this training camp?"

I could see that she wouldn't be making this decision lightly. I needed back up. It was useless to keep begging. I figured that I still had time to convince her. Training camp didn't start for a few weeks, so there was no point in getting upset yet. Besides, she respected Mr. Holt, (considering he was our teacher last year, albeit briefly!) and I was sure he'd be happy to meet with my parents. Even though it was Katia's suggestion that I should be admitted, he had approved the idea, so he must have thought I was up to the challenge!

I promised my parents that I'd get them a meeting with Mr. Holt as soon as possible and then I headed out for a surf. I knew that I needed a plan of attack if I was ever going to be allowed to go to Protector Training Camp. Hopefully, Jet and Allie would have some ideas for me. I grabbed my surfboard from the doorway and flew off to meet my friends.

Since moving to Byron Bay, we'd all learned how to surf. The humans were addicted to it, and the Water Fairies had developed their own unique way of surfing that's so much fun. It's out of this world. We have surfboards just like the humans, BUT we attach the board to our feet so that we can ride both the waves and the wind. It's a mix of flying and surfing and it's our new obsession. Jet is a natural, of course, and it's become a bit of a daily ritual. There's a whole new industry in Byron Bay for fairy surfboards, and guess who the hot new designer is?

Allie!!!

She's really found her niche here. She designs surfboards and swimming togs for all the local fairies and has become the most in-demand designer on the East Coast. Her parents have even set up a shop that they run for her, and it's so successful that they do it for a living now. Allie does the designs and they handle the orders and the accounts. After everything she went through last year (being captured and held prisoner by our King), it's good to see her so happy.

"Hey guys, how's the surf today?" I asked them.

"Come on in LOLA, there are some nice clean breaks and there's a pod of Bottlenose dolphins out by the lighthouse. If you're lucky, you might see them!" shouted Allie.

"Race you," challenged Jet as I jumped on my board and skimmed across the top of the waves to meet them in the water.

"Where are we racing to?" I laughed.

"Last one to the Lighthouse and back has to get the ice creams," answered Jet.

"Deal," shouted Allie and I, and then we were off.

"Hey cheats, I didn't say go," puffed Jet, as he raced to catch us.

Determined to beat Jet for once, Allie and I sped off. We could feel him breathing down our necks as we surfed off huge waves high into the sky and then coasted on the wind, bopping and diving up and down on the tops of the waves.

As we neared the lighthouse, I could feel Jet was hot on my heels. Allie had slipped behind and I could hear her moan in frustration as Jet overtook her. Argh, not today Jet, I thought. Today victory is mine, I thought, and I gritted my teeth and focused on the turn ahead. This was where he often overtook me. If I chose the wrong wave or made a bad turn, he'd have me. I saw a huge clean wave roll out to the right. I figured that if I jumped on that and let it spit me out to the left, I'd be back on track in the other direction and ready for the home stretch.

"Yes!" I cried as I hit the wave perfectly, flipped 180, and rode it into shore. Jet was hot on my heels, but for once, he had to admit defeat.

"Well to be fair, you did have a head start," he said.

"Come on, you must admit that I had you on that last wave," I replied.

"Smashed him LOLA, nicely done," Allie high-fived me as she pulled up next to us on the beach.

We all sat down, red-faced and laughing, as Jet continued to protest about being robbed.

"Did someone say ice cream?" I nudged him cheekily. Jet begrudgingly agreed to go and get some, much to our surprise. Jet does not like coming second.

Whilst he was gone, I filled Allie in on my conversation with my parents. Her parents were so supportive of her dreams to be a designer that I hoped she might have some suggestions for how to win mine over.

"You know LOLA, I can kind of understand why they're hesitant. I must admit I'm a bit worried too," she said.

"Why, don't you think I can handle it?" I asked her.

"It's not that LOLA, I know you can handle the training. I suppose I'm being selfish, but I just want you here with us. You were gone for so long last year, and it was hard not seeing you or knowing what you were doing. I imagine it was torture for your parents," she added.

"Thanks for being a caring friend, Allie, but it's different this time," I reassured her. "You'll all know where I am and who I'm with. Jet will be there and Mr. Holt is a trainer, so it's hardly the same thing," I reasoned.

"I know, but you need to understand that it's a big decision for your parents. You'll be gone for three months at least, and then who knows if you'll come back at all. I've heard that they use this training camp to recruit full-time Protector Fairies. If you get chosen for that, we might never see you again!"

Allie looked down at the sand and drew circles in it as she talked. I could tell that she was worried about me not returning, and I hadn't thought of how my decision might affect our friendship. I made a mental note to make sure nothing got in the way of it, because she's too important to me to neglect.

"Allie please don't be sad, I can't stand it when you're upset. I promise I'll stay in touch and it's not like I'm a million miles away. The camp is literally thirty minutes from here and we can arrange visits. Anyway, it might never happen. I need to get permission from my parents first." I replied glumly. I realised that I might have been kidding myself and would perhaps have to wait another year before my parents agreed to let me go.

"You've got a point with the distance. Thirty minutes is pretty close, and I suppose we can use it as practice for our telepathy skills," said Allie in an effort to cheer me up. "Mr. Holt being an instructor there is a big plus. Why don't you ask him to talk to your parents? He's an adult and he was a school teacher for a while after all," suggested Allie.

"I was thinking he'd be my best bet. I'll go and ask him today, no time like the present," I replied with a renewed sense of hope.

"Ask who what today?" said Jet, as he handed us our coconut ice creams.

"MMMM coco-raspberry, my favourite," I replied. I was suddenly distracted by the delicious ice cream dripping down my hands and making them all sticky.

"I'm going to ask Mr. Holt to talk to my parents about Protector Training Camp," I managed to say, through mouthfuls of runny ice cream.

"You mean they haven't said yes yet?" asked Jet.

"No, I think I'm still in the bad books. How did you convince your parents?" I asked, hoping that Jet might have some words of wisdom.

"It wasn't easy but I've been working on them for a while. Mr. Holt suggested it when he was training me last summer and he's been over to our place for tea a few times, which helped. I think my Mum has a soft spot for him," Jet chuckled. "Dad didn't seem to notice, but he seems happy that Mum's happy. So there you go. Either way, it worked. They asked him how much it would cost. When they found out it was free, and that I still had my school lessons, they signed me up right away! They were probably glad that I'll be someone else's problem for a few months," added Jet with laughter.

"Well, I hope it will be that easy for me. If I can't convince them, I'll be gutted. I'll go and see Mr. Holt today. Do you know if he's still living at the surf club?"

"Last I heard, he was staying with some other Protector Fairies until training camp starts. They've got a few wooden beach shacks under the surf club on Main Beach," replied Jet.

Allie and I sat and finished our ice creams in silence, whilst Jet wolfed his down and headed back out into the surf to catch some more waves. My head was full of reasons why I should be allowed to go to camp. I had one shot of convincing my parents that I was ready for this, and that I wasn't too young and would make them proud. I had to play it smart and keep my cool this time around. Getting angry and storming off would not help my case. I had to make them see that this was the BEST possible thing for me to do in my life right now. Mr. Holt was the key; if I had him on my side, I was sure I could make them see sense.

Later that afternoon, I flew to Main Beach and went looking for Mr. Holt. I could see the big human surf club standing tall and impressive in the sand, but I couldn't spot the wooden shacks that Jet had told me to look for. I circled the whole building and found nothing, so I decided to sit and wait in the hope of spotting Mr. Holt. The beach was full of people having fun, children building sandcastles, and water lovers splashing about in the sea, diving under waves and jumping on surfboards and boogie boards. I also saw teenagers kicking footballs around and girls braiding one another's hair.

It never ceases to amaze me how we fairies can live side by side with humans, yet most of them have no idea that we even exist. I would never have dared to sit out in the open like that in the Blue Mountains. The King had us scared of our own shadows, encouraging us to hide and live in secret. The truth is that humans are so caught up in their own lives that they pay hardly any attention to the world around them. I often fly right past them, right in front of their faces, just to see what will happen. Mostly, they don't bat an eyelid. Sometimes they will swat me away thinking I'm a fly. Every now and then, someone will stop and stare for a second wondering what they just saw, before quickly convincing themselves that it was nothing or just a figment of their imagination. It's amazing really. Once you have a few tricks up your sleeve (which I now have plenty of), you can have some real fun with humans.

I was lost in thought so I didn't notice Mr. Holt arrive. He tapped me on the shoulder and I jumped up ready to defend myself.

"Whoa LOLA, I come in peace," laughed Mr. Holt as he backed away in mock fright.

"Sorry Sir, reflexes you know…you could have been anyone!" I replied with a giggle of embarrassment.

"Good to see you're staying sharp. It's true that you never can be too careful, but I think you're pretty safe here, don't you?" he asked smiling kindly at me.

"Yes Sir, actually I was here waiting for you," I told him.

"Ah, were you now. Well what can I do for you?" he asked.

"It's my parents, Sir, they won't let me go to Protector Training Camp… well, they haven't said no exactly, but they are asking all sorts of questions and they're very nervous about it. I was wondering if you wouldn't mind talking to them, you know, as a teacher and an adult. I really think they'd listen to you, and I will just DIE if I can't go. Please Sir, say you'll talk to them!" I begged.

"Phew, take a deep breath LOLA. Of course I'll talk to them. I was planning to do that at some point anyway. I just wanted to give your parents some time to think about everything, considering what they went through last year. I can't promise anything though LOLA. At the end of the day, they are your parents and they have every right to say no if they don't think you're ready.

"I did warn you, thirteen is still very young for this type of training camp. You'll be the youngest student ever to be accepted and it will not be without its challenges. If it weren't for your heroics last year, the powers that be wouldn't even consider taking you, but… well enough of that. I know you deserve your chance and I can see your potential, that's for sure…"

He paused.

"I'll do my very best for you LOLA. Leave it to me and I'll let you know how it goes."

"When Sir? Can I come with you? Maybe we could go right now? I know they're at home," I urged.

"I'll go and see them tomorrow, and I'd prefer to see them alone LOLA. I don't want you to get upset if they say no. There's always next year after all," he added, laughing kindly.

"But Sir," I began to say, and then I thought better of it. I knew he was right and I decided to trust him. I just had to hope and pray that my parents would trust him too.

"Thanks, Sir, I really appreciate it," was all I said in reply and I turned to head home.

Mr. Holt nodded and waved, looking a little surprised that I had given in so easily.

After dinner, I made my excuses and went to bed early. A lot was riding on the outcome of the next day and I didn't want anything to spoil my chances. I went to sleep with all my fingers and toes crossed, eager to discover what my future would hold.

17 DAYS AND COUNTING

After a tense day of fidgeting and worrying, worrying and fidgeting, Mr. Holt finally went to see my parents and, lo and behold, he won them over!! I had no idea how he managed it, especially since I had felt certain they would say that I was too young to attend this year.

But no, I was going to Protector Training Camp. It was official! Of course, there were some very strict rules that my parents insisted I agree to:

Rules for Training Camp

- Leaving the training campgrounds without a teacher present is strictly forbidden
- Paying attention in ALL my classes NOT just my favourite ones
- Strictly no fighting outside of lessons
- No trying out new powers unless instructed by a teacher
- No crazy adventures unless supervised by a teacher
- Other rules I can't remember
- *Blah blah blah*

…But I didn't care, they could give me a hundred rules if they wanted to. All I heard was YESSSSSS!!!!

Praise the sun and the sea and the waves and the seagulls, life was throwing me a bone and I was going to grab it and run like the wind. The hardest thing now would be getting through the next month while I waited for camp to start. Isn't that always the way? The days before a big trip seem to drag on and on forever.

"Guys, guess what?" I gasped, as I found Allie and Jet polishing their surfboards in Allie's shop.

"No idea, but you look excited, so that can only mean one thing. He did it… am I right? He convinced your parents to let you go to training camp!" guessed Jet, his eyes wide open in anticipation.

"You guessed it, meet your new training buddy!! Mr. Holt is a dead set legend and that's a fact!" I beamed.

"I'm really pleased for you LOLA, but I'll miss you. I'll miss both of you," said Allie, struggling between being happy for her friends and feeling sad for herself.

"It's not so far away Allie, and it's only for three months. You can come for visits on the weekend and like you said, we can practice our telepathy skills. It will go by so quickly, we'll be back before you know it," I promised her.

"I suppose so. But who will I hang out with while you're both gone?" she asked.

"What about Paige and Eva, they adore you already! Plus there are heaps of awesome Water Fairies you've still got to get to know. You know heaps of surfers now through making your boards, and they'll all be dying to hang out with the best surfboard designer in town," I assured her.

That seemed to cheer her up a little bit. Paige and Eva were the first Water Fairies I met when I arrived in Byron Bay last year and they had really taken me under their wing - back then I had no idea that I had so many magic powers and they helped me to master them. I knew they'd be great friends to Allie too in my absence. Allie smiled and gave me a hug.

"I'm really happy for you. I know you really wanted this and I'm dead proud of you LOLA. Being the youngest fairy to go to Protector Training Camp, that's a pretty big deal!" she said, beaming with pride.

"I can hardly believe it myself, this is the next step on my big adventure. I can't wait to learn some new magic powers and finally be able to beat Jet in a fight!" I laughed.

"Yeah right, dream on LOLA. Remember, I'm going to camp too, so I'll learn everything you learn and I'll make sure to always be one step ahead. You're pretty good, I'll give you that, but I am the master and don't you forget it!" said Jet, as he puffed up his chest and spread his wings as wide as they would go.

"You two seriously, I don't know who is worse!" said Allie rolling her eyes.

"Come on then Allie, show us your latest boards," I encouraged her. I knew she'd been working on some new designs and I wanted to take her mind off the fact that we would be leaving soon.

"Well, now that you mention it, I do have a few new designs I've been working on. It's part of my *Rebels & Warriors* range. In tribute to all the brave animals that helped us last summer, I wanted to do something to show them how important they are to us. You know, kind of a thank you, so each animal gets its own surfboard design. What do you think?" Allie pulled back a big sheet that was covering a row of ten surfboards. Each had a beautifully illustrated animal as the main feature, surrounded by graphic swirls and shapes in bright neon colours. They were simply stunning!

"These are awesome Allie, I bet every fairy from here to Bondi will want one!" said Jet, choosing a bright blue board with a dragonfly emblazoned across it.

"Can I give it a whirl? I've got a big surf competition coming up and I'd love to surf on your board, if you'll let me," he asked.

"Sure, that would be awesome. The boards haven't been tested yet, so the edges might need smoothing down before this one's competition ready - let me know how it handles," said Allie to Jet as he grabbed his new board and headed out to the waves.

"LOLA, pick out your favourite one. You can have whichever one you want!" offered Allie excitedly.

"Awesome, thanks!" I answered and swooped in to grab a purple board with a gorgeous sea turtle on it.

"I'll come with you. I've done enough work for one day, and now it's time for play!" cried Allie as she grabbed a pink board decorated with a cockatoo grinning back at her.

We flew off towards the surf and forgot everything as we dived headlong into the waves. Lost in the tumble of surf and wind, we played for hours and then watched as the sun came down on another stunning day on the coast of Byron Bay.

The next two weeks passed by without incident. My parents were getting used to the idea of me going away and were even planning a few adventures of their own. They admitted that they had always quite fancied a big trip around Australia and with me being away for three months, they thought it might be the ideal time to do it. Of course, I was totally in favour of this idea. The farther away from camp they were, the less likely they were to interfere with my training or to fuss about what I was up to. It helped that Jet's parents were also planning a trip to see relatives in New Zealand and were quite vocal about how this was their big chance to have some fun too!!

Jet and I spent a lot of time talking about what we expected to learn at training camp. The truth was that we didn't know much about it - what with it being a heavily guarded secret and all - but we managed to come up with a list of possible things that we might learn. Okay, so maybe I wrote the list and Jet begrudgingly agreed to sit there whilst I read them to him...

Things We Might Learn at Camp:

- How to time travel
- How to stop time
- General stuff about time & travel
- Making humans forget things we want them to forget
- Making humans see things we want them to see
- General things about controlling humans
- Super strength, like Mr. Holt has
- Fighting skills, and how to beat anyone with just a few moves
- Advanced protective shields ~ maybe there are different kinds of shields for different situations?

There were heaps of other skills we thought we might learn, but we agreed that our list contained the most likely ones. Of course, we also knew that we'd have to get much better at the powers we already had first. We hadn't had much reason to practice our skills since last summer, and to be honest, we were having so much fun surfing and enjoying our new life at the beach that we'd all been a bit slack in our training. We agreed that we'd better get some practice in before we went to training camp, or we might look amateur compared to the other recruits. We made a pact to practice one skill every day until we left.

The little I had heard about being a Protector Fairy made it seem like the best job in the world. It was widely considered to be the most important job that a fairy could do - outside of being a Queen or a King. You see, our world was constantly under threat of being revealed. Even though living in fear and limiting our powers like our previous King encouraged was NOT the answer, we still had to be careful. After all, we fairies have a big job to do and we can do it better if we fly under the radar. The job of a Protector Fairy is to protect the planet and all the fairies and creatures living on it. Whilst I didn't really know HOW we were supposed to do that, I was sure we'd find out at training camp, and that it would be epic!! It's the most respected job in the world for a good reason. Everyone knew that if you did well at training camp, you were pretty likely to get offered a full scholarship at the Protector Training Academy, so I needed to stand out and show them what I was made of.

The countdown was on, in just 17 days, Jet and I would be on our way to camp and all would be revealed. Hello destiny!!

THREE

STIFF COMPETITION

The annual Malibu Classic surf contest was one of the biggest events on the Byron Bay calendar for humans, and this year the Water Fairies had decided to get in on the action by hosting a fairy-only version!

Jet was primed for a win. Even though he was new to surfing, everyone agreed that he was a natural. Proudly surfing on one of Allie's new boards, Jet was feeling super-confident and was ready to rock the waves. The swells were big and everyone was excited to see the best of the best battle it out to be the ultimate champion.

I was excited for another reason too. Katia and the Water Fairies had told me about a pod of dolphins coming in to watch the contest. Apparently, they were bringing their new baby calf and I'd never met a newborn dolphin before, so I was pretty keen to meet her.

"LOLA, you're here already. How's Jet doing?" Katia swooped down next to me with Banjo buzzing close behind. * *Dear reader, Banjo is an adorable bumblebee and is pretty much a fixture in our lives - he's a wicked DJ, makes up raps for most occasions and is useful in a battle as I found out last year.*

"Hey LOLA, what's happening?" asked Banjo, slurping noisily on a honeydew slushie.

"Hey Banjo, hey Katia. Not much, we're just waiting for the competition to start and checking out the locals. It's quite an impressive turnout. Is it always this busy?" I asked them.

"Yep, this is one of the main events of the year for humans. The swells are super big in May, so we should see some impressive surfing. I hope Jet's up for it, he's only a newbie to surfing after all!" said Banjo smiling.

"You know Jet. He loves a challenge and is super competitive, so I'm sure he'll give it his all," I answered confidently.

"What about you LOLA, are you not entering the competition?" asked Katia.

"Maybe next year, I don't want to show Jet up!" I giggled.

"Hehe, well, in that case, why don't we go and check out the rest of the beach. There's plenty to see. I've set up a pretty neat viewing platform right by the front so when the competition starts, we will have the perfect spot to watch Jet show off," said Katia, and she motioned for me to follow her into the crowd.

It still felt really risky to me being out in the open so boldly. I wondered how long it would take me to get used to it. Katia flew confidently ahead of me as if she were invisible, and I supposed, if we wanted to, that we could have used our powers to make ourselves invisible too. But Katia insisted that there was no need. "Why would we waste our energy?" she reasoned.

I was so lost in my thoughts that I hadn't noticed what was going on around me. I came to an abrupt stop when I nearly flew right into Katia, who was hovering and pointing excitedly out to sea. I followed her gaze and was amazed to see a pod of dolphins jumping playfully out of the water, blowing out huge gusts of air and spinning in the waves. The whole beach had stopped to watch them. The humans were taking pictures and exclaiming loudly at witnessing such a beautiful sight. Children giggled in delight, grabbing their parents and begging to be lifted up onto shoulders so that they could get a better view.

We flew out to meet the dolphins, skimming across the tumbling waves and feeling the utter joy of the wind in our wings and the salt spray on our faces. When we reached the dolphins, Katia introduced me to them and I did my best to remember each of their names.

Delphine was the leader; she had a beautiful smile and several scars on her fins, one of them was so badly clipped that it looked like a fork. Her eldest was called Sly, and he was the biggest of the bunch by far, he was relatively unscarred with jet-black fins and was at least four metres long. When he jumped up out of the waves and came crashing down, he made a huge splash, much to his delight. He seemed to enjoy showing off for the crowds. Her youngest was the newborn, Milly. She was staying as close to her mother as it was possible to get and was a bit scared of us - which I found funny considering our size. Three other adult females (Connie, Francis and Bo) circled close by, ready to help out Milly if she got into any trouble. They uttered reassuring clicks and squeaks that I understood to mean, "It's okay, these fairies are our friends."

"I'm so glad that you made it today," said Katia to the dolphins, beaming. "I wasn't sure if you'd make the journey with Milly being so young."

"You'd be surprised! Don't let her shyness fool you, she's learning quickly and is already proving to be quite self-sufficient. I have to keep my wits about me with this rowdy bunch, I can tell you," laughed Delphine.

To a bystander, the sounds would have seemed quite strange. A lot of high-pitched clicks and squeaks, but both Katia and I could understand the dolphins quite clearly - it was like this with all creatures. We could hear both what the humans could hear, such as birds chirping and bears grunting but we could also hear their words. I have no idea how it works – it's a mystery to me still. But the easiest way to describe it is someone who can speak two languages. We can speak to and understand humans but we can also speak to and understand birds, insects, animals and fish.

As I played a game of peek-a-boo with Milly, Katia continued talking to her friends. "Are you staying to watch the surf competition?" she asked them.

"We will stick around for a bit, for sure. I've never seen fairies surf in a competition before, so that's definitely worth watching. But we can't stay all day, because I've got two little sick ones being looked after by their Dad near Wategos Beach. I don't know what's bothering them, but they have gone right off their food and are complaining of terrible tummy pains," said Delphine.

"Oh no, that's no good at all. Do you want me to take a look at them for you?" asked Katia kindly.

"Thanks Katia, that's very thoughtful of you, but I'm sure they will be fine. Hopefully, they will feel better tomorrow and if not, I'll come and get you. I'm sure it's just something they ate. You know what growing boys are like, they eat anything and everything," she replied.

"Okay, if you're sure, but it's really no bother. You know where I live anyway, if you need me," said Katia.

"It's showtime!" squawked a seagull, as he swooped dramatically past us.

We looked up to see flocks of seagulls descending on the beach. That could only mean one thing: feeding time. It is a well-known fact that seagulls love to eat human food. They have plenty of their own food to eat, but they just love fish and chips, preferably battered and covered in ketchup. Go figure, seagulls just love ketchup. Whenever you see a large flock of seagulls moving at great speed, you can be sure that they are headed towards food. Sure enough, the humans were making their way across the beach to watch the surfers compete, and many of them were leaving behind their lunches half eaten or barely touched. The seagulls were circling overhead and perched nearby, ready to pounce on the discarded feasts. As the large bell rang and signalled the beginning of the competition, the loudspeakers sprang to life and announced each contestant. The seagulls were busy stealing chips and fighting over leftover morsels of battered fish. They were making quite a mess!

We took this as our cue to go to the viewing platform, ready for the fairy competition to start. The plan was to closely follow the human competition. The theory was that the humans would be so involved in their own show, that they most likely wouldn't pay attention to the other end of the beach where our competition was taking place.

"Hop on ladies, get ready for an extreme ride back to shore," Sly motioned for us to grab onto his fin.

I looked over at Katia to follow her lead - I'd never been on the back of a dolphin before. Without hesitation, she jumped onto Sly's back, grabbing a hold of his fin and standing up with her legs bent and wings pushed back ready for action. I copied her stance, took a deep breath in and braced myself, not knowing what to expect. Then we were off.

Sly dove head first under the waves. The shock of it nearly threw me off, but I clutched onto his fin with all my might and closed my eyes as we plunged underneath the water. The ocean never ceases to amaze me, once submerged it's as if you have entered a whole new world. The sun's rays shoot through the surface, turning fish into dazzling flickers of neon orange, blue and yellow. All around me the Dolphins spun and twirled, tutting and clicking to one another and turning the sea into a soda stream of bubbles and sparkling lights.

I whooped for joy as we broke through the waves and met the fresh air. Water streamed off Sly's back and rushed past us. We laughed and clung on for dear life as Sly spun a full 180 degrees out of the water. He wasn't kidding when he said it would be an extreme ride. All too soon, we were slowing down as we approached the shore.

"This is where I leave you ladies, I hope you enjoyed the ride," said Sly cheekily.

Katia laughed, "I can see what you mean Delphine, you sure do have your work cut out for you with this one. I can tell he can be quite a handful," she chuckled.

"Hey, I'm right here," said Sly, pretending to be offended.

"Sorry Sly, we are grateful for the ride, aren't we LOLA?" prompted Katia.

"We sure are, thanks Sly. That was AWESOME!" I shouted, still quite hopped up on adrenalin. Everyone laughed as I made Sly promise that he'd take me and my friends out one day soon. I couldn't wait to tell Jet and Allie about this. Jet would be so mad that he missed out. Suddenly I remembered why we were there in the first place and that my friend would be competing soon. I would kick myself if I missed it.

We said our goodbyes and promised to catch up again over the next few days whilst the dolphins were staying nearby. They headed back out to sea, where the waters were deeper and it was easier to swim and play. Katia and I made our way over to the viewing platform, which was already packed tightly with fairies jostling for a position. It was quite a scene, so many beautiful wings and brightly coloured outfits fluttering in one spot. To the humans, it would have looked like a swarm of beautiful butterflies had descended onto the beach. I spotted Allie hovering with Paige and Eva and I made a beeline to join them.

"LOLA," cried Allie as I approached, "we were wondering where you'd gone, the competition is about to start any minute now."

"Does anyone know the rules?" I asked them.

"Apparently, it's done in rounds," answered Paige. "There are three rounds, so that's three chances to impress the judges. Each surfer is marked on how many waves they catch, how big the waves are and how long they stay on them, plus any tricks they do whilst surfing. There is an element of luck involved, but the most important thing is knowing which waves to surf and which waves to let pass by. If the surfers jump on a small wave too soon, they might miss out on catching a bigger one later."

"Thanks Paige," I replied. "Has anyone spoken to Jet yet? I wonder if he is nervous."

"I haven't spoken to him," answered Allie, "but I've seen him messing about in the waves all morning, doing flips and stuff. He's with that new surfer friend of his, Eddie I think his name is. They haven't left the water all morning, so they don't seem too stressed to me. I think Eddie's competing too, that's how they met."

"Sounds like Jet, I hope he's kept some energy for the main event," I laughed, knowing full well that he'd be fine - one thing Jet was not short on was energy.

"Well I guess we'll find out now," said Allie, as a huge gong went off and we rushed towards the front of the platform to get a better look.

Eight fairies lined up on the shore, and I noticed six of them were carrying Allie's boards. "Have you seen that Allie? You're famous!" I whispered excitedly. Allie squeezed my hand in acknowledgement and we waited nervously for the bell to ring, signalling the start of the first round. Jet was on the far right. He was dressed in a dark blue wetsuit cut off at the knees and was clutching his neon blue surfboard. As the bell rang, he sprinted out to sea and used his board to propel him out. He was neck and neck with two other surfers when they finally settled out at sea and sat waiting for a good wave. It wasn't long before the first surfer spotted a promising wave and decided to ride it. He was the only one who jumped on his board, so we watched as he made the best of it that he could. Sadly for him, the wave never quite reached its potential and he dropped off it before being able to do any tricks. Frustrated but not defeated, he swam back out to join his fellow surfers and wait for a better wave.

We collectively held our breath as we saw a large swell begin to build. It came from the right, rolling in behind Jet and I could see that he was preparing to surf it. Just as it reached him, Jet sprang to life and rode majestically on its curve, the water rolling and breaking around him as he surfed in a perfect tube of water. Not content with just cruising, Jet spread his wings and flicked himself a full 180 degrees so that he was surfing the wave completely inverted for a while, (much to the crowd's delight). The wave eventually tapered off and Jet was pushed gracefully into shore. I could see a huge grin spread across his face, so I knew that he felt confident in his first attempt. Three other surfers, including Eddie, had caught the same wave and also followed it into shore. I had no idea how well they had ridden as I was completely absorbed watching Jet, so I could only hope that Jet had some more tricks up his sleeves. After two more uneventful waves, the bell signalling the end of round one rang. All the surfers made their way back to the beach for a quick break. Jet and his new friend seemed quite happy to stay in the water. Whilst everyone else was getting a drink and checking their boards, Jet and Eddie were doing handstands in the sea by the shore.

Round two saw only seven of the original eight surfers head back out to sea. Jet was the first one out again, however, it was his friend Eddie who stole the show in this round. Whilst Jet

managed to ride an impressive three waves in short
succession, Eddie picked a beauty and navigated it perfectly:
surfing the barrel, flipping on top of the crest, then flipping
back to finish inside the barrel as it rolled into the shore. Jet
and Eddie high-fived each other, whilst surfing side-by-side on
their boards. The crowd cheered them on, as they back-flipped
into the sea, laughing and fooling around the whole way.

As we nervously waited for round three to start, it was still
too close to call. I knew Jet was doing well, but I had no idea
how the judges were marking them or who was in the lead.
Eddie was a good competitor and there had been at least two
other standout moments for other surfers in the competition.
Even though I was completely focused on Jet, I could hear
roars of approval going on around me for other surfers, so I
knew that it would be a tough one to judge. It all rested on the
final round. I knew how much winning this would mean to Jet,
so I really, really wanted him to win.

The bell sounded and the surfers pushed out to sea again.
The crowd was silent as we waited with bated breath for the
waves to form. We were so absorbed that we had completely
forgotten that we were sharing the beach. I looked around to
see that the humans were watching their competition with just
as much relish. The beach was alive with kids and parents
cheering on their favourite surfers. Are we really so different
from them after all? I thought to myself. Allie nudged me and I
snapped my head back around just in time to watch Jet take
off on a huge wave. This one was menacing. In fact, I could see
that he was struggling to stay in control of it as the wave
tumbled and growled, chasing him and nipping at his board
with the threat of throwing him off. I've seen humans eaten up
and spat back out by gnarly waves. Granted, Jet had the
advantage of being a fairy, so he was a bit more capable than a
human - but he could still be caught off guard. I could tell this
wave was challenging him on every level. Just when it looked
like he would be swallowed up, Jet grabbed his board with
both hands and rolled a full 360 degrees inside the barrel until
he was surfing perfectly inside it, he was buried so deeply

inside the wave that we could hardly see him but somehow he managed to surf it safely all the way back to shore.

We collectively breathed a sigh of relief. Allie let go of my hand and I realised that we'd been gripping each other in fear. I could hardly feel my fingers. As Jet surfed back to shore, the crowd roared and he theatrically raised both hands and bowed before dismounting with a cartwheel. Such a performer! Eddie followed closely behind, so he must have caught the same wave. All we could do now was hope for the best.

"Wow that was certainly something, wasn't it?" grinned Allie.

"You can say that again. I think I need a lie down to recover and I didn't even do anything!" exclaimed Eva.

"It certainly makes for exciting viewing. I've watched the humans compete for years and that was just as exciting," added Paige.

"When do we find out who the winner is?" I asked Paige, as she seemed to be the most informed on what was happening today.

"I'm not sure, but I think it will be soon. If it's anything like the human surf competition, they just need to check the scores and will then announce it pretty quickly, I would imagine," she answered.

"Where's Banjo?" I asked, suddenly aware that I hadn't seen him since that morning. Banjo was normally at the centre of any fun event, and I couldn't see him missing out on this.

"He's setting up the decks for the party tonight," Paige reminded us.

"Ah, of course, I completely forgot," I replied, remembering now that Banjo had been working on his set list all week, "I hope he still caught the action."

"Don't you worry about Banjo. There's no way he would have missed that, I'm sure he was watching nearby. Are you sticking around later for the party? The humans normally kick on until the wee hours, so that will keep them busy here. Katia has promised to put a glimmer *(a magic charm)* over our entire cave and the whole shoreline around it, so you can expect quite a spectacular setup. The theme is *An Octopus's Garden*, like the famous song!"

"What? Nobody told us there was a theme. I would have made costumes!" cried Allie, genuinely distressed. She loved any excuse for a dress up party and there was not much time to make outfits now.

"Sorry Allie, honestly she only decided today. Katia does that sometimes. Don't worry we're all pretty good at glimmers around here and you can help out too. It will be good practice for you both. Besides, you can camouflage yourself to be whatever you want to be, remember?" Paige reminded us.

Allie and I both grinned as we realised that she was right. We could easily whip up a costume from some seaweed, shells, and plants and with our new camouflaging skills we could be anything that we wanted to be. My mind started turning over the choices. I quite fancied the idea of a seahorse or maybe an electric blue Jellyfish...and as my hair was a lovely shade of neon blue I thought I could do a pretty convincing impression of a blue jellyfish.

My thoughts were interrupted by a deep horn blast that signalled the judges were ready to announce the winners. The crowd buzzed with excitement as they waited for the results.

"Attention please, if we can have a little quiet. Thank you for coming out today. That was the first in what we hope will be an annual event for our community, and I think you'll all agree it was a big success!" said Noel, the Fairy Surf Club Manager. "I know you're all keen to get ready for the party, so without further ado, I will read out the results... In third place, with an impressive 24 points, is Sammie!"

We all looked around to see a blonde haired girl called Sammie rush to the front and receive her trophy.

"In second place, with an almighty 27 points, is Jet!"

Oh no... my heart fell for Jet. I knew he'd be a little crushed, but I hoped he'd still be proud of himself. Second place is still awesome, and there was no doubting how well he had surfed those waves, especially the last one. Whoever beat him must have been ah-mazing. We watched as Jet went up to receive his trophy. He held his hand in the air in thanks, and I was really pleased to see a big grin on his face. I was relieved that he was taking it well.

"And the winner today, with an unbelievable 28 points, is Eddie!"

The crowd went wild. Obviously a crowd favourite, Eddie looked quite shocked to have won. "Speech, speech, speech," chanted the crowd. Eddie nervously accepted his trophy and, still looking quite stunned, turned to look at Jet.

"I thought this was yours for sure," said Eddie, to which Jet answered, "No way man, you completely ripped it up today. You deserve to win."

I was so proud of Jet. I knew that he was secretly gutted that he didn't win, but he hid it well. He was the perfect sportsman, picking up Eddie like a champion and parading his friend down the beach to huge roars of applause from the crowd.

"Well, that wraps it up for today everyone. Congrats to Eddie, our first Annual Surf Comp Champion, and thanks to all the surfers out here today. You were all amazing competitors and we thoroughly enjoyed the show," said Noel. "Now before you go, remember to leave nothing behind. If everyone takes what they brought with them, we should leave no mess. The humans will do a beach cleanup but not until tomorrow. That still leaves a lot of time for rubbish to end up in our oceans. Katia asked me to remind everyone that we will be doing a beach cleanup before dawn, so please join us. We need as many volunteers as possible."

We made our way back to our caves, ready to transform ourselves for the party. I hadn't been to a party in Byron Bay yet. I wondered if it would be as much fun as I'd been told.

FOUR

AN OCTOPUS'S GARDEN

Allie and I got to work the minute we got back to Allie's cave. We had just under two hours before the party started, so we eagerly began creating our costumes. All around us, we could hear fairies frantically preparing for the party - stages were being built, decorations were being hung - whilst they chatted excitedly amongst themselves.

Allie decided to go as a lobster. She had a big shell to cover her back and was working through a range of glimmers for her body and her wings - it was so much fun to watch her as she tried to get the colours just right. We decided to play a game to test out our new powers; I called out an animal, insect or a sea creature and Allie tried to camouflage herself to become it as quickly as possible. Then she called one out for me and I had to do the same. The hardest part was visualising it in the first place - unless you had a really clear image in your mind of what you were trying to become, it was very hard to get it right. One mistake and you would end up looking like a weird mix of things. Much to my delight, Allie kept getting her vegetables and her animals mixed up, so her prawn looked more like a carrot and her ladybird looked like a strawberry.

"Stop laughing LOLA," cried Allie in fits of giggles. "Okay your turn. I want you to be a cockatoo, and you've got 30 seconds - go!" She pointed at me as I quickly tried to conjure up a convincing cockatoo in my head. I found it easiest to try and remember a real one, one that I'd met - that seemed to work the best for me. As I concentrated, I felt my body shimmer and shake and I felt the familiar tingling sensation as I magically transformed. My chest and head swelled to become bigger and bigger, I could feel my legs stretch and a weird itching sensation covered my body as I sprouted feathers all over. Once I was sure that my transformation was complete, I opened my eyes and looked at Allie, waiting for her reaction.

"Spot on LOLA, very realistic. You're really getting the hang of this. From a distance, I would totally believe that you are a cockatoo. I wonder how long it lasts?"

Actually, I had no idea. I made a mental note to ask Katia how long it was possible to stay transformed. Maybe this was one of the things we'd learn at Protector Training Camp.

"Good question. I know one thing though… it's really itchy being a bird. It must take some getting used to, having all those feathers. I think I'll stick to something less scratchy tonight," I giggled. "Go on, give me another one then," I challenged Allie.

We wasted at least an hour taking turns becoming sea creatures and animals, and it seemed I had quite a knack for it. To be fair, I had had a lot more practice than Allie, and anyway she was such a great dressmaker she didn't really need to glimmer herself in the first place. I eventually settled on an electric blue jellyfish. I'd spotted a magnificent one just last week off the coast, so I had a vivid image in my mind to work with. Allie whipped up some long flowing neon blue tentacles for me, made out of silk and covered in ink blue seashells. Once I'd attached those to my newly glimmered body, I could be mistaken for the real thing. Allie did a great job of being a lobster. The huge orange shell on her back and two massive pincers attached to her wings were the main showpieces, and her pink and beige camouflaged body with shimmering pearl pieces gave just the right hint of the soft flesh inside her shell. Her little face looked hysterical as it beamed out from underneath her heavy load.

"Are you sure you aren't going to topple over in that Allie?" I laughed, thinking that maybe she'd gone too far in her efforts to be convincing.

"No I'm fine, if I get tired later I can always take off the pincers," she replied, as she began chasing me around the room with her comedy-sized claws.

"Back off or I'll sting you," I warned her, now laughing so hard I was crying.

"I can hear you two giggling from a mile away," said Jet as he popped his head around the corner into Allie's room. "Cool outfits. Let me guess… Allie, you're a heavy duty looking prawn and LOLA you're an octopus," he guessed.

"Cheeky! I'm a jellyfish and Allie is a lobster," I told him, hoping he was joking as I thought we looked exactly like a jellyfish and a lobster.

"Not bad, not bad at all. What should I go as, any ideas?" he asked us.

"A shark, definitely a shark," replied Allie. "I've got just the thing. Come back here with me and put this on," she said, while handing him a dark grey and black wetsuit. It was complete with a full head cover, some flippers and a fin from a surfboard that doubled perfectly as a shark's fin.

"Too easy, thanks Allie. I didn't even have to glimmer," said Jet, chuffed to bits with his outfit and the fact that it required zero effort from him. "You're the best."

"I know, I know, what would you do without me?" said Allie grinning.

"Let's go and join the others in getting the room ready," I suggested.

We made our way out into the main cave. The cave was always an impressive sight, but I wasn't prepared for the vision I saw before me. Katia and the other Water Fairies had certainly been busy. In the past couple of hours, whilst Allie and I had been playing dress up, it had been completely transformed into an underwater garden. Bubbles rose slowly from the ground, travelling up to the roof of the cave and then back down again. The floor was covered with sand and seashells and the walls were alive with swaying coral and underwater plants. The entire cave was bathed in blue and silver lights that twinkled and danced, giving it the impression of being part of the ocean. We watched as Katia turned her attention to different parts of the room, transforming it in front of our eyes. A group of ten Water Fairies hovered on each floor of the cave applying glimmers to the 200 houses contained inside. As we walked away from Allie's home and looked back at the doorway, we saw that it now appeared to form one part of a huge shipwreck. The window had become a porthole to the ship and scattered treasure including gold and jewels lined the doorway.

"Wow, they weren't kidding. Katia sure knows how to glimmer a room!" I said to a stunned Allie and Jet, who nodded in reply and continued walking around admiring everything. "How can they possibly have done all this in the time it took us to get ready?" asked Allie, clearly impressed.

"No comment," said Jet, laughing.

"What are you trying to say? We were quick today," reasoned Allie.

"Nothing, I've just known…" But Jet didn't get to finish his sentence. All of a sudden, a Water Fairy rushed past us, closely followed by two more. They had grave looks on their faces and were headed straight for Katia, knocking Jet sideways as they flew past him. They whispered something to Katia and we watched intently as her face fell and she immediately turned to follow them back out of the cave.

Something was wrong.

I tried to read Katia's mind, but "Delphine" was all I heard.

The room suddenly felt dark and sinister, as if the magic and beauty of the glimmers were leaving along with Katia.

"Katia, what is it, what's wrong?" I asked as she rushed past us.

"It's Delphine. Her children are in trouble. I need to get to her quickly," she shouted as she flew out of the cave and into the dead of night.

"Let's go," I said to Jet and Allie.

"But what can we do?" asked Allie. "She didn't ask us to go with her, what if we are in the way?"

"She didn't tell us not to go either," I answered. "We can just go and find out more information, I'd rather be there if she needs us."

"I agree," said Jet as he took off his fin and flippers, "Allie you can come too or you can raise the alarm here. Try and find Paige and Eva, Katia will want them there," added Jet.

"I'll get out of this gear and then come and find you. I won't be any good to anyone in this get-up. I don't want to slow you down. You go quickly and when you get there, show me the location using your mind. I'll try and find Paige and Eva in the meantime and we'll meet you there as soon as we can."

"Okay follow me, I know where Delphine and her pod are," I said as I flew off in pursuit of Katia.

A sense of dread filled me as we flew into the night. I had no idea what was waiting for us, but I couldn't shake the horrible feeling in my bones. I hoped I was just being my usual dramatic self, but something urged me on and told me to be quick. I followed my instincts, flying on pure adrenalin, nerves jangling and tentacles streaming behind me. I'd completely forgotten that I was dressed as a blue Jellyfish, what a strange sight I must have been.

As we approached Wategoes Beach, we scanned the seas looking for any sign of dolphins or fairies. Sure enough, we spotted a circle of fins - just off to the right in a secluded bay. They were dangerously close to the shore. I could see Katia circling the water furiously in one spot and I could sense her urgency. Jet and I exchanged a worried look and made a beeline right to her. In no time at all, we were hovering above the scene and could see what was causing such distress. Two beautiful dolphins had washed up on the shoreline. One was writhing in terrible pain, struggling to breathe, and the other was completely still...deadly still. Delphine was arching and flipping in distress and Katia was muttering something I could not hear, holding her hands out towards one of the dolphins. She was concentrating all her powers on the poor dolphin writhing in agony. I tried to take in what I was seeing, but the distress of Delphine and her baby Milly was unbearable. I felt a huge pull towards Delphine and concentrated all my energy on calming and soothing her. I was struggling to come to terms with what I was seeing. Delphine had lost one of her children, and her other boy looked gravely ill. I felt powerless to do anything and desperately hoped that Katia could save him.

"Monster," muttered Milly as if in answer to an unasked question.

"What do you mean Milly?" I asked, quite confused.

"It must have been the Ocean Monster," she said, quite clearly now.

"Shush now child," said Delphine, stroking her little one with her fin and nudging up against her, "there's no such thing."

Ocean Monster? I thought, what a weird thing to say. I wonder who put that idea into her head. Probably one of her older brothers or sisters to scare her... At least it seemed to have distracted Delphine from her anguish for a minute. I looked over again at Katia and saw that whatever she was doing seemed to be making the poor dolphin worse, or at least it looked that way. He was bucking and rocking on the shore, opening and closing his mouth and making the most terrible gut wrenching noises. I couldn't bear to see him in such pain, but then he heaved and heaved and spewed up an almighty amount of water and nasty stuff onto the beach. After that, he calmed down and the pained expression on his face relaxed a little bit.

Katia fell back onto the sand exhausted from her efforts. Delphine ventured as close to the shore as she could without risking beaching herself and fussed over her son as he slowly recovered. Once she was sure that he was out of danger, she rubbed up against her other son - who lay silent and unmoving in the shallow waters. She made the most heart-wrenching sounds – only someone who has lost someone so precious would understand. As I watched Delphine morning the emotions I felt were raw and powerful. Part of me wanted to flee and disappear from that place altogether whilst another part of me wanted to kick and scream and punch something in anger.

"I'm so sorry Delphine, it was too late for him," said Katia through tears.

"My beautiful boy. Why didn't I allow you to take a look at him earlier? It's all my fault, if only..." wailed Delphine.

"Now now, don't do that to yourself," said Katia, flying down to be by Delphine's side. "There was no way you could have known that a stomach ache would lead to this," Katia assured her.

"What about Dylan, will he be okay?" she asked pointing to her other son, who was thankfully swimming now and slowly venturing a bit further out from the shore.

"He will be fine, I promise you. Whatever it was that caused the sickness, it seems to be out of his system now, so he'll only get better from here. He just needs lots of rest and TLC," replied Katia softly.

"What do I do now? I can't just leave him here, he'll be all alone," whispered Delphine, motioning to her poor departed son, Ryan.

"It's up to you Delphine, would you like to bring the rest of the pod in to say their goodbyes?' asked Katia gently. "Then we can help you move him out to sea and give him a dignified farewell."

Delphine nodded her head slowly and resumed wailing as the realisation dawned on her that her boy was really gone. We watched as she grieved the loss of her beautiful son. Katia flew out to where the rest of the pod was anxiously waiting for news. As they made their way into shore, the overwhelming waves of sadness and grief were more than I could bear. I motioned to Jet and we flew off to wait nearby on a hanging tree on the hill, letting the family say their goodbyes in privacy. I remembered that I'd completely forgotten about Allie. I reached out to her with my mind, explaining what had happened as best I could and telling her that it was probably best if everyone waited for us at the cave. I asked her to let everyone know that the party was cancelled. There was no way we would be celebrating that night.

Eventually, Katia made her way back to us. There was nothing more she could do to help and Delphine and her family were heading back out to sea to start the long grieving process. We flew back to the cave in silence. Our hearts were heavy and tears blurred our vision.

"My friends," said Katia, addressing the entire Water Fairy community. "As you may have heard, tonight we have suffered a terrible loss. A beautiful dolphin named Ryan sadly passed away on the shores of Wategoes Beach. His younger brother Dylan thankfully survived, but I'm afraid that we were too late to help Ryan. You all know Delphine and her family. They have been regular visitors to these shores for many years. Please join me in a few minutes of silence. I ask that you send out love and condolences to Delphine and her beautiful family in their time of sadness."

After a few minutes of complete silence, Katia addressed us again, "As I'm sure you will all understand, the party tonight is cancelled out of respect. Try to get a good night's rest."

We all nodded and sadly made our way back to our own homes. My parents were waiting for me at the front door, the news having reached them earlier. My Mum pulled me in close and hugged me until I could barely breathe, then my Dad circled us both in his long arms and squeezed even harder. I stayed there crying until I ran out of tears and then I went to my room.

~

After four days and nights of barely leaving my room, Katia came to see me.

"LOLA, I've come to see how you are feeling," she asked me softly.

I wasn't sure that I wanted to talk to her. I couldn't help feeling like we should have done more to help Ryan, we should have insisted to Delphine that we go and see him.

"I've thought those exact same thoughts LOLA, believe me, but there is nothing that anyone could have done," she replied, obviously hearing my thoughts. This was the only annoying thing about mind reading. Fairies like Katia that are super in tune can read your every thought... you had to be very careful about controlling your mind.

"I just can't seem to shake it, I feel so sad all of the time... How can I just go back to being normal and doing everyday things when I feel like this?" I asked her.

46

"LOLA, it's completely normal to feel as you do, and you must allow yourself to feel the emotions," said Katia softly. "Death is a natural part of life and it can't always be avoided I'm afraid," she continued.

"I feel like I'll never be happy again..." I told her sadly.

"I know it feels that way now, but with time everything heals. The way I see it, right now you have some choices to make. You can either choose to stay inside your room and keep yourself closed off from those who love you and care about you... or you can choose to go outside, get some fresh air and talk to your friends who are all worried about you," said Katia. "Come on, this isn't the LOLA I know. The LOLA I know picks herself up and faces things head on, even if they are hard."

"Maybe that LOLA doesn't exist anymore, maybe I've changed?" I challenged her, honestly thinking that some part of me was broken for good and it couldn't be fixed.

"Sorry, I just don't believe that LOLA, and I know in your heart that you don't believe that either. Please listen to me and trust me, you will feel better soon. This is certainly not the last time that you will witness death, and it will always be a terrible thing to go through. Allow yourself time to be sad, that's okay, it's natural, but talk to your friends about it and talk to your parents. Don't lock yourself up alone in your room, that won't change anything. You always have a choice LOLA. You can stay here and cling onto your feelings of sadness like a blanket or you can go out and face the day and see what it has in store for you. Life goes on LOLA."

I looked up at Katia with tears rolling down my face. She wiped my face and smiled the most beautiful smile I'd ever seen. I felt so loved and accepted in that moment that I could feel my bruised heart starting to heal.

"Now come on, let's go outside. Let's get some air into those lungs of yours and then I'll take you to your dancing tree. That's your special place and I know that it's exactly where you need to be right now." Katia motioned for me to follow her.

I nodded and followed behind in her shadow, stretched out my wings and took off.

JADE HARLEY

FIVE

MYTHS AND LEGENDS

The dancing tree was dancing up a storm as we approached. Its strong trunk was rooted deep beneath the earth whilst its long branches reached out to me in a welcoming embrace. It was exactly where I needed to be. Katia sat in silence next to me as we watched the sunset over Byron Bay and then sensing that I needed some time to think, she left me alone. The leaves and branches rustled all around me, and I felt safe there as I rocked softly, held in the tree's strong arms. I focused on the sensations around me, like the wind whistling through the leaves, the warm glow of the setting sun as it touched my skin and the smell of smoky barbeques sizzling away below. I remembered what Katia had said to me earlier and I realised that she was right - life goes on...

For some reason, I was reminded of what Milly had said on the beach that day. 'The Ocean Monster did it...' what had she meant, I asked myself. How could I find out without upsetting Delphine and the other dolphins? Maybe there was something to it after all. I knew what it felt like to be ignored just because you were young - maybe she knew something we didn't. The least I could do was investigate, after all I reasoned, it couldn't do any harm.

I headed back home with a renewed sense of purpose in my belly. If there *was* an Ocean Monster, I wanted to find out what it wanted and why it would hurt an innocent creature like Ryan. My mind was bursting with questions as I flew home. I felt more like myself than I had in days. I had a new mission.

"LOLA, we're so glad to see you out and about, we've been so worried about you," said Paige, hugging me tightly.

"We've missed you heaps LOLA, are you okay?" asked Eva, looking concerned.

"I just needed some alone time, that's all. I didn't mean to worry anyone," I replied. "Hey, can I ask you both a question, confidentially?" I whispered, quickly changing the subject.

"Sure, of course you can," replied Paige.

"Have you ever heard of the Ocean Monster?" I asked them, anxiously waiting for their answer.

"Ocean Monster?" asked Paige, "like for real?"

"Yeah I know it sounds weird. It might be nothing, but the little dolphin, Milly, blamed the Ocean Monster for hurting her brothers... at least I think that was what she was trying to say..."

"We were told stories of an Ocean Monster when we were kids growing up," answered Paige. "But it's just a myth, an old legend told to make kids respect the power of the ocean. It's not real."

"Well, how do you know it's not real?" I asked.

"No one has ever seen it LOLA," said Eva. "I used to be terrified of that legend when I was a kid, but like Paige says, it's just an old story."

"Humour me. Tell me how it goes..." I asked her.

"Okay, so the myth goes that there's an Ocean God and he controls the oceans, the waves and all the creatures in the sea. As long as we respect the oceans and all the life in it, he will be happy and leave us in peace. BUT, if we disrespect his kingdom, he will turn into a Monster that grows larger and larger until one day he will flood the lands and kill everything in his reach," said Paige.

"And you believed that when you were kids?" I asked.

"Sure, most of us did. It's partly why we go and help out at every beach cleanup. It's important to keep the seas clean as a sign of respect," explained Paige.

"But the seas aren't clean. You should have seen the amount of rubbish that came out of poor Dylan when he threw up. His belly was full of plastic," I answered.

"Well in that case, if there was an Ocean Monster, he'd be angry by now and surely we would have seen him..." reasoned Paige.

"I suppose you're right, I'm probably just letting my imagination run wild. Crazy story though, no wonder you were scared as kids. Imagine if there WAS an Ocean Monster and he got really mad... scary stuff..." and I shivered at the thought.

"Hey, what are you doing right now?" asked Eva.

"Nothing, just heading home. Why?"

"Well, a few of us are having a get together at my place. We do it once a month and it's kind of like a storytelling club. You should come along! If you like myths and legends, we've got loads of crazy stories for you. You'll love it!" urged Eva.

"Okay sure, why not. Have you seen Jet or Allie today? Can I invite them too?" I asked. "Allie is worried about Jet and I going away to Protector Training Camp, so I think it would be great for her to make some new friends before we leave."

"Sure, the more the merrier," replied Eva.

I used my mind to see where Jet and Allie were...

"Nice work LOLA, I can see you're practising your mind reading powers. I always laugh when you go rushing off to talk to someone when you could just as easily use your mind. I wonder how long it will be before your powers become like second nature to you," said Eva, laughing kindly.

"I know, it's so weird. It's like they still don't really belong to me. I'm guessing that I'll get to practice them more at Protector Training Camp," I said. In the back of my mind, I wondered why the skills were still so foreign to me. Because I had spent most of my time with Jet and Allie, and we had known each other for years before recognizing these powers existed, we still tended to do things the same way. I hoped my familiar habits didn't get me into trouble at camp, I thought.

"I'm sure they'll understand," replied Eva, reading my mind. "I've got an idea actually... we can help you out tonight by making it a silent storytelling club!" she suggested excitedly.

"Great idea Eva!" said Paige, getting excited by the thought of it. "Yes, tonight no one is allowed to talk at all. Everyone has to tell their stories using their minds only, and that way you'll learn to have multiple conversations at once," she replied.

"I don't know. That sounds a bit hectic to me, how will I know who to listen to?" I asked - it sounded quite complicated.

"Don't worry, you'll get the hang of it. We'll take it slowly, and it will be fun!" promised Eva.

By now I had locked onto Jet and Allie. Allie was working away on her drawings at her desk, no doubt designing the latest hot sensations for fairies far and wide to wear. Jet was in his room practising his kicks in the mirror and thinking about training camp. I asked them both if they fancied joining us. At first, I could tell that they were surprised to hear from me (especially since I was using my mind), but they quickly replied and agreed to meet us. We all made our way back to Eva's house - she was on the top floor with an amazing view that looked straight out onto the beach. As I stopped to peer out of the huge windows, a large red crab wandered past. He looked me up and down and then (clearly deciding that I was no threat) moved sideways past the window, giving us a quick nod of his head in acknowledgement. Living in a cave by the sea means getting used to the strangest of neighbours.

The inside of Eva's room could only be described as an underwater palace. Everything was fancy. The window frame was covered in pearls and glistening jewels, the ceilings were draped with meters and meters of different coloured silks, and there was a four-poster bed made out of wood with dramatic carvings of mermaids decorating the frame. The finished effect was quite splendid.

Eva watched me take it all in with an open mouth. "I know, I know, my Mum is kind of a 'more is more' person, if you know what I mean," she said, obviously a bit embarrassed.

"No not at all," I answered hurriedly, as I hadn't meant to offend her. "I'm just taking it all in, it's so stunning!" I said, genuinely impressed with the effort her Mum had obviously gone to.

"Yeah, Mum loves to glimmer. Come back next week and she'll have completely changed it again, it's what she does.... I have to check the door number each time I come home to make sure I'm at the right house..." she giggled nervously.

"Well, I love it, and I feel like I'm in a Princess's bedroom," added Allie. "Where should we sit?" she asked.

"Make yourself at home, hop up on the bed. I'll get some fruit and some snacks - we can have a picnic. The others should be here soon," she replied, looking at Jet, who was clearly feeling outnumbered by all the girls.

"I might go and find Eddie, see what he's doing," said Jet, as if on cue.

"Really, you don't want to stay for a bed picnic?" I asked him while giggling, knowing full well that a bed picnic with a bunch of girls was Jet's idea of torture.

"I'm not hungry, I'll catch you guys later," said Jet as he blushed and hurried out of the room.

"Oh well, more for us then," exclaimed Eva as she served up a plate overflowing with delicious treats and plopped it on the bed directly in front of us.

"Yum! You've got my favourites... peanut butter cups," exclaimed Allie as she dove in and grabbed one.

"Paige, can you organise some music, please? If it's going to be a silent party, then we might as well put some good tunes on, what do you think?" asked Eva, looking up at her friend expectantly.

"Sure, do you want background music or sing-along music?" asked Paige.

"I think it's safest to stick with background music tonight," answered Eva. "LOLA and Allie are new to this. Mind reading with multiple people is hard enough as it is, without having to sing along to music at the same time!" she said, not realising how nervous all this talk was making me. I looked over at Allie who looked just as worried as I was.

"Girls, girls stop stressing," said Paige. "It's just a bit of fun, I promise that even though it sounds difficult, it's not that hard once you get into the swing of things. It's just like having a normal conversation - we talk over each other all the time anyway..." she reminded us.

"Where are my ladies at? I'm here!" sang Sasha as she entered the room. I'd seen Sasha around but we had never been introduced. She was the most over-the-top looking fairy I had ever seen, she glided into the room like she was a movie star and she looked like one too. She smelled of roses and jasmine, and the room literally filled with her scent.

"Sasha, yay, you made it," cried Eva as she rushed over to hug her friend. "Sasha, this is LOLA and this is Allie," she introduced us proudly.

"I have heard all about you girl," gushed Sasha as she made a beeline straight to Allie. "You're the new designer right? I've seen your stuff girlfriend, it's like shizam hot!" she said, much to Allie's delight.

"Thanks," blushed Allie in surprise, "I can make you something if you like."

"Really, I'll have to take you up on that, I saw the cutest little swimsuit you made for my friend Maddy, and I just have to have one!" she exclaimed excitedly, sitting down right beside her.

I don't like to think of myself as the jealous type, but I admit that I was a bit jealous. This Sasha girl with her flaming red curls, her green eyes, and her big personality had zeroed in on my best friend and seemed determined to steal her from me. I'm embarrassed to say that I didn't like her, not one bit! I tried my hardest to think nice thoughts. This was not the night to be getting jealous…not when the whole room was going to be reading my mind… focus LOLA, focus! Allie and Sasha continued talking about dress styles and trends the humans were wearing, and I tried to keep myself calm and focus on anything but Allie and Sasha chatting like they'd known each other forever. By now a few other Water Fairies had entered the room. There was Annie and her friend Chen, who were happily discussing the benefits of bathing their wings in honey, which I personally had never heard of. Then there was Scotty - the only boy in the group - who quickly made himself useful by making everyone name badges and writing a list of suggested conversation topics on the wall – ah a fellow list maker! He had twinkly green eyes and a dimple on his chin, I liked him immediately.

Paige banged a gong and the room fell silent.

"Ladies, and Scotty," she smiled to Scotty, who curtseyed in mock delight.

"Welcome and thanks for coming. Tonight we have some new friends I'd like to introduce to our little storytelling group along with some new rules..." she added, which seemed to pique everyone's interest. "This is LOLA and this is Allie," said Paige gesturing to us on the bed. We both waved and blushed as everyone gave us the once over. I was suddenly really keen to make a good impression, so I smiled as much as I could without looking goofy.

"As you all know, our little group is committed to keeping alive the old myths and legends of the fairy world. For those of you who haven't met them, LOLA and Allie moved here from the Blue Mountains and they don't know much about our history, they certainly don't know any of the old stories that we grew up listening to. Plus, they were never taught how to communicate using just their minds... so we thought if you'll all play along tonight, we could kill two beetles with one stone..."

Dear reader, this was just a figure of speech of course. Everyone knows that fairies would never kill beetles - or any other living thing for that matter.

"We will tell LOLA and Allie some of the oldest stories that we know BUT silently, using only the power of our minds to communicate," instructed Paige excitedly.

The whole room was totally buzzed, they all agreed and then argued about who would go first. Scotty charmed the room and was given the first rights to tell his story. I kept one eye open and watched the room - keen to see everyone's faces as they concentrated on using their minds to communicate.

"Once upon a time a long, long time ago," began Scotty theatrically, "it is said that all fairies, us included, were once in fact just plain old humans. There were no magical creatures at all, the earth was dark and barren with very little life and the humans that did exist were sad and miserable. The Gods of the Land, sick of witnessing such a miserable sight every day, decided to do something about it. So they took tiny amounts of their own powers and bestowed them on a few chosen humans just to see what would happen…and surprise, surprise fairies were created!" said Scotty triumphantly.

I tried to follow him using only my mind, but I couldn't resist sneaking a peek at the faces of my fellow fairies. They were all enthralled (all except Sasha, who seemed more interested in plaiting her long hair and sneaking glimpses of herself in the mirror). I closed my eyes again and concentrated hard.

"The humans that became fairies had the power to bring light and happiness to the world and they set about their task with vigour. The Gods were impressed by how quickly the fairies transformed the earth - plants flowered, trees grew, animals multiplied and there was harmony. The Gods, who had other worlds to deal with, decided to entrust fairies with the ongoing protection of the earth and every living creature on it. BUT they made it known that if the fairies failed, if they could not preserve harmony and keep the earth healthy, then the fairies would be turned back into humans and that their fate would be linked to the humans. If the humans were wiped out, then the fairies would be too…" finished Scotty with a flourish.

"Huh, what a load of nonsense!" interrupted Sasha, forcing herself into our heads.

"Hey, watch it you, I believe that one!! I happen to take my mission on this earth very seriously, unlike some of us, who are more interested in looking good…" replied Scotty angrily.

"There's nothing wrong with looking your best," shot back Sasha.

"Of course not, but it shouldn't be the only thing filling that head of yours, there are more important things to think about you know…" replied Scotty.

"Hey, hey, be nice, both of you," said Paige. "I promised LOLA and Allie that we'd take it slow. This is their first time having a group mind conversation, keep the squabbles to a minimum please," added Paige, giving Sasha and Scotty a stern look.

After all that back and forth, I felt a bit dizzy. I opened my eyes and was relieved to see that everyone else had their eyes open too. We looked expectantly at Paige, who it seemed had been deemed the leader of this weird little get together. She took a deep breath and we all copied her.

"Now who wants to tell the Ocean Monster story? LOLA asked me about this one earlier today, so I feel it's only fair that she gets to hear it tonight. Who wants to volunteer?" asked Paige looking around the room.

I silently thanked her. I was hoping that I'd get to hear the full story tonight. My heart sank as Sasha jumped up and down begging to tell us. I tried to hide my disappointment and remind myself that I wanted Allie to make new friends, so I should be nice to Sasha. I couldn't understand why I had taken such a disliking to her, after all it wasn't like she'd done anything to me. Other than the fact that she was clearly an egomaniac and she was trying to steal my best friend!

"Sasha, the stage is yours," said Paige.

"Okay, so this story starts a long, long time ago before there were humans OR fairies on the planet," began Sasha, projecting her voice and vivid images into our minds. I concentrated on her words and tried to quieten my mind, because I really wanted to hear this story. "The Ocean God was the first ever ruler and some say he is the strongest and the most powerful God of all. He once controlled the whole planet, covering it with water and he was the master of every living creature. The other Gods, who were jealous of his power, bargained with him - they gave him jewels and golden treasure in return for half of his kingdom - which they then turned into dry land. The Ocean God watched on in bemusement as the other Gods carried out their great experiment, allowing humans and animals to multiply and entrusting fairies with the future of the earth. He swore to keep this bargain as long as his Kingdom was not affected by the carelessness of humans. So when a storm rages out to sea and the tides swell, it's believed by many to be a message from the Ocean God to heed his warning or he'll flood the land and reclaim it as his own," finished Sasha theatrically.

I was completely absorbed in her storytelling. I had to admit that she possessed a clear strong voice and the images that she projected into my mind were very lifelike. I decided to try harder to like her; if she was going to be Allie's friend, maybe she could be mine too. I opened my eyes and smiled warmly at her, that wasn't so hard now, was it? I thought to myself. I decided to try and ask her a question using my mind, no time like the present after all.

"So, has anyone ever seen the Ocean Monster?" I asked her, making sure to include everyone else in on the conversation as well.

"There have been rumours, sure," she answered, pausing dramatically. "On particularly stormy nights, some have claimed to have seen him, but it's just a far fetched tale. A story told to keep little children respectful of the sea and to stop them from littering. Of course it's not actually true," she added smugly. "Everyone knows that we have been around far longer than humans and there is no evidence to support any of these myths."

"How can you be so sure?" I asked her. "Think about it … if you asked a human sitting out on that beach today if fairies exist, they would say no, right? Well, what makes this any different?" I asked.

I was met with stunned silence.

I opened my eyes to see if anyone was talking and I was missing it, but everyone was deadly silent. Oops, what had I done? Trust me to say the one thing that I probably shouldn't say. I couldn't resist. I knew I should zip it but the words kept tumbling out of my brain.

"I mean seriously, think about it: Who says we came before the humans, that's just a story too right? Who knows whether there is or isn't a bunch of Gods sitting there watching everything we do. All of it is a question of belief, isn't it?" I was getting excited now - I loved nothing more than a good debate.

"Humans think we are just a myth, a fantasy, make-believe, whatever you want to call it...but we all know that we are not! Does their lack of belief in us make us any less real? No. Well then, who's to say that these stories about the Ocean Monster aren't based on some facts? I think it's very short-sighted of us to completely disregard them without investigating for ourselves first," I finished, opening my eyes and waiting to see their expressions.

"Well, welcome to the storytelling club LOLA! I must say, that goes down as the most interesting 'getting to know you' session yet. I think you're completely bonkers, but I LOVE the enthusiasm!" giggled Scotty breathlessly. He beamed around at everyone, trying to gauge their reaction to my rant. I remembered in embarrassment that I hardly knew some of these fairies, and I could see them looking at me strangely. Even Paige and Eva looked momentarily lost for words and they were sort of used to me by now.

Paige saw me blush and kindly stepped in, "You raised some very good points LOLA, I have never really thought about it like that before. I honestly don't have any answers BUT what I can say is that tonight was very successful on the mind communication front. You all managed to keep silent, and the conversation never faltered, not even for one minute. So well done everyone, especially Allie and LOLA, what with it being your first time and all," she said beaming.

I was so completely absorbed in the stories being told and the gazillion questions running through my head that I had forgotten it was being conducted in complete silence. Paige was right. Once you got into the swing of things, it was almost the same as having a regular conversation. I also realised that I hadn't felt sad all night. I was proud of myself. I was leaving tonight with more questions than I came with, but at least I'd nailed one thing! I could now add complex mind reading and listening abilities to my ever-growing list of skills. Katia was right, life doesn't happen if you lock yourself away.

FIVE ROUNDS WITH JET

I dreamed about monsters and strange happenings that night. I woke up feeling disorientated and confused, not knowing what was real and what was folktale. My dream had felt so real that it had taken me a few minutes to snap back into reality and realise that it was just a bad dream.

In my dream, I was living with the Water Fairies - but instead of living in the cave, we lived deep under the water, in a place not unlike the Octopus's Garden that Katia had glimmered for the party that was never-to-be. I had the strangest feeling of being chained down as I watched my friends and all the creatures of the sea go about their daily business. I was witnessing the scene going on around me, but I had no ability to affect it - like I was trapped inside a glass box. Out of nowhere, a huge creeping blob spread through the water all around me, it was black and jellylike in substance and was swallowing everything in its path. I couldn't tell what it was - because it certainly didn't look like any animal or creature I had ever seen before - but I could feel its rage and anger. Worst of all, I could tell it wasn't going to stop. Everything it came into contact with it smothered and ate whole, leaving behind nothing but a sea of black jelly. I was powerless to stop it. I fought hard against my chains, desperately trying to break free. The blob got closer and threatened to swallow me whole too... then I woke up.

I did not like that dream, not one little bit.

At breakfast I told my Mum about it, and I wondered if she'd ever heard of a black blob like that.

"A black blob, no I've never heard about a black blob LOLA. You say the strangest things sometimes, where do you come up with it all?" she laughed at me as she cut up some fruit for our breakfast. "It's just your imagination playing tricks on you LOLA. That would be all those myths and tall tales they told you last night, you shouldn't listen to such nonsense," she assured me.

"You're probably right. It just felt so real and I was powerless to stop it," I explained.

"Well it was just a dream, a weird one I'll grant you that, but nothing to get too upset over," reasoned my Mum. "Now eat your breakfast, it's not long before you go to training camp and I want to feed you up a bit before then."

I did as I was told and tucked into my breakfast; my appetite had come back now that I wasn't feeling so sad all the time. My Mum was right, I would definitely need my strength for training camp. I was already a bit worried. I had hardly trained at all, and last week was a complete write-off. Jet had begged me to go surfing and training every day and I'd completely blown him off. I wasn't in the mood. But something about the black blob dream had reminded me how terrible it feels to be powerless. I never wanted to experience that feeling ever again.

I needed to train my body and my mind to stand up to any challenges I might face and there was no time to waste! So this time when Jet knocked on the door, I surprised him and my Mum by jumping up and joining him. Neither of them said anything, but I could tell by the quick look they exchanged that they were happy that I was acting like my usual self again. The best thing about Jet was that I didn't need to explain myself to him; he just got me.

"Thanks for not making a big deal out of things," I said, and left it at that as we flew off towards the dunes. He could easily have been annoyed the way I'd been blowing him off recently.

"That's cool LOLA, I get it. I knew you'd come around eventually, you always do," he said matter-of-factly.

"Well thanks, it means a lot. I feel a lot better now. Katia made me realise a few things. But I need you to seriously kick my butt into gear if I'm ever going to be ready for training camp. At the rate I'm going, I'll be well behind the other recruits. I'm already the youngest, I refuse to be the weakest as well," I told him.

"LOLA they wouldn't have accepted you if they didn't think you were up for it. Sure you might be the youngest, but you're also one of the bravest fairies I know. I mean it. There are not many fairies who would go against all the odds to save their loved ones like you did. You're a hero as far as I'm concerned. Plus I hate to admit it, but you have a seriously good kick on you! Let's train, Mr. Holt is waiting for us. You are a born Protector LOLA, and don't you forget it," said Jet.

I grabbed him in a headlock and kissed the top of his head as he shouted in protest. I was a lucky girl to have such a great friend in my corner.

"Ding ding, round one," said Jet cheekily as we hopped into the ring Mr. Holt had set up for us. I bowed to Jet, and we both grinned like maniacs before getting to work. I bounced around the ring, feeling the blood rush to my face. I watched closely as Jet jabbed, testing my reactions, and I ducked and weaved as he threw a left jab and then a right cross. He left himself open, so I brought my knee up high and delivered a front kick straight to his belly. He flew back and hit the ropes, momentarily winded and called for a time out.

"Okay then, someone came meaning business today... what was all that about not being ready?" he laughed at me.

"Are you okay?" I asked. I hadn't realised how hard I had kicked him, I just knew that it felt good to be back in the ring again. I felt alive.

"I'm fine, you just caught me off guard that's all. Ding, ding round two," said Jet as he set his stance and got ready to rumble again. I loved this about Jet, when it came to fighting there were no hard feelings. When we were in the ring, it was purely business. We both brought our best to the table and whoever won, won. It was as simple as that.

We danced around the ring for another five rounds, and by the third round we'd gathered quite an audience. Jet's friend Eddie was cheering him on, seemingly enjoying being his wingman, patting down his face and giving him a drink of water in between rounds. I had Banjo in my corner - he was a big fan of kickboxing and was supplying some interesting rhymes at each interval. Naturally, he was a fan of the famous line *float like a butterfly, sting like a bee*, but he had adapted his own version. If I remembered correctly, it went a little something like this...

Jet can't touch what he can't see
Float like LOLA and sting like me
LOLA can't lose with me on her side
Jet better run cos there's nowhere to hide

At the end of the fourth round, we were neck and neck, Jet had won two rounds and I had won two. I was feeling bruised and exhausted, but alive. I hadn't felt this good for soooo long. I had forgotten how much fun this was. We faced up to each other as Mr. Holt rang the final bell.

"Ding, ding."
I jumped straight in and caught Jet with a nice uppercut. He bounced right back at me, surprising me with a kick to my knee. We danced around the ring, jabbing and kicking, spinning and exchanging punches. So far neither of us had a clear lead, and then I stepped in at just the right moment and caught him with a spinning elbow. It connected with the side of his head and made him stumble into the ropes. I saw him wobble and adrenaline flooded my body. Now was the time to finish him, so I gave it everything I had. I was relentless, letting out my anger and sadness with every punch. Jet absorbed it all, covering up as best he could as I continued to rain down punches. The bell rang and I slumped into a heap on top of Jet.
"Feel better?" he whispered into my ear as I collapsed in relief. We lay side by side in the ring, panting and recovering as everyone around us cheered.
"LOLA, LOLA," chanted the crowd.
"Jet can't touch what he can't see
Float like LOLA and sting like me," chanted Banjo.
"I think we can safely say that you won that one... but I'll get you next time," said Jet as he pulled me up to meet my fans.

"You know LOLA, I haven't seen someone fight with that much determination in a long time. It's a good thing you both had headgear on!" said Mr. Holt as he approached the ropes.

"Jet good effort, but it seems LOLA just wanted it more today," he said, shaking Jet's glove.

"I don't know what she had for breakfast Sir, but I'm going to ask her Mum for some of it tomorrow," he laughed.

"It's good to see you both practising, I haven't seen you train for a while," said Mr. Holt. "I'm looking forward to welcoming you to camp, and get ready to be pushed hard, the pair of you," he added winking. "LOLA, you'll have to teach me that spinning elbow, that was beautiful to watch."

"Thanks, Sir," I replied, grateful for his praise. "Do you think I'm really ready Sir, honestly? I know I'm the youngest, but I don't want to make a fool of myself..."

"LOLA, that question I cannot answer. Do I think you are ready? Yes of course I do, I would not have approved it otherwise, and I certainly wouldn't have convinced your parents to let you go. But YOU need to KNOW that you are ready LOLA. Surely today shows you that you have what it takes physically... now you need to be ready mentally. Great things come to those who expect them LOLA, remember that."

How did Mr. Holt always know exactly what to say?

Great things come to those who expect them... I liked that.

SEVEN

A TURTLE'S TALE

After training, Jet and I decided to cool off in the waves. It was such a beautiful day and the deep blue sea was calling us. I could not wait to dive in and feel the cool water soothing my aching bones. Eddie came with us, but I didn't really mind as I was starting to enjoy his company. The more questions I asked him, the more intriguing I found him. For instance, when I told him about the stories I'd heard about the Ocean God, aka the Ocean Monster, he had simply nodded and said that he'd heard all about the Ocean Monster from a bunch of turtles that he hung out with on the regular. Just like that.

"Yeah there's an old fella, a sea turtle called Samson, I met him when I was surfing last year in Queensland. He told me some stories about friends of his who had actually seen the Ocean Monster and then mysteriously died shortly afterwards," said Eddie matter-of-factly.

"What do you mean they died shortly afterwards, what did they die of?" I asked.

"He didn't know, that's what was so strange about it. The turtles were all pretty healthy and then they started getting sick one by one. They started floating for no reason and couldn't dive down for food. They starved to death in the end. It's like they lost control of their bodies and what used to come to them naturally … weird right?" said Eddie.

"Really weird, I wonder what could make them do that? Was it some kind of spell?" I asked, searching for a logical explanation.

"I don't know but they swore to Samson that they saw the Ocean Monster and then the next thing you know, within days of supposedly seeing it they were dying. I can't see why they'd lie about such a thing but don't go spreading that around. You're the first person to take me seriously," said Eddie thoughtfully.

"Popular opinion isn't always right you know," I assured him.

"You can meet him if you like, ask him for yourself," said Eddie.

"Who, Samson?" I asked excitedly. "Really? I'd love to meet him. Where is he?"

"He's swimming with his hatchlings not far from here. If we grab our boards and head out past the lighthouse, I'm sure we can find him," he replied, motioning for Jet and I to follow him.

We grabbed our boards and paddled out to sea. The shore disappeared behind us until the humans playing on the beach looked like tiny insects. Jet and I hung back on our boards whilst Eddie tried to find Samson. It wasn't long before we spotted a bale of sea turtles headed our way - some of them were clearly hatchlings, furiously trying to keep up with the big turtles that were leading the way.

* Dear reader, please read the following conversation between Eddie and Samson in your best Australian accent for your reading pleasure.

"Eddie mate, what's happening, bro?"

I assumed this was Samson. He seemed clearly stoked to see Eddie.

"Not much dude, just chillin'," replied Eddie grinning. "I wanted you to meet some friends o' mine, this is LOLA and this is Jet. LOLA was asking about your mates that died. I told her the yarn about the Ocean Monster and she's keen to hear it."

"D'ya mean they don't know about the Ocean Monster?" asked Samson in surprise.

"Nah bro, they grew up in the mountains, like all secluded 'n' that. They're only just learning about all this stuff ay. Anyways you know what it's like, I get laughed at when I say the Ocean Monster is real, no one believes me ay..." said Eddie dejectedly.

"More fool them. I know what I saw and it weren't natural," replied Samson. "We haven't been back to the deep ocean since it happened, proper shook us up it did," Samson turned to lock eyes with me, I returned his gaze and gave him my full attention.

"All I can tell you is what they told me ay. They said they saw it on a stormy night, the waves were gnarly and the rip was pulling 'em backwards. They saw a dead-set giant object moving in the tide, it spread itself out and oozed across the ocean, turning everything around 'em murky and black. They said it felt like the waters were infected with something evil and they didn't feel safe ay, so they swam as far away as they could, but the feeling o' fear never left 'em."

"Did it have a face? Did it talk to them?" I asked Samson.

"Nah, that's what they said were strangest of all. It was more of a feeling than anything, they just knew it was bad joo-joo and had to get away. Have you ever just had a feeling LOLA down deep in your gumboots?" asked Samson.

I remembered all too well what that felt like - the feeling that something wasn't quite right was exactly what set me off on my adventures last year.

"Yes. Yes, I have," I nodded in reply. I had that same feeling again now. It was like there was something I was supposed to do...but I didn't know what. First, there were the dolphins, now these poor sea turtles. What was killing them? I wondered. Had we somehow angered the Ocean God and turned him into the way scarier Ocean Monster? One thing was certain, I had to get more information.

"What about you, have you ever seen or felt anything unusual?" I asked Samson.

"Nah, like I said, I just saw what happened to me mates and I don't want that happening to me or me little'uns, I know that much."

"I hear you," I replied. "Well thanks for sharing your story. If you hear of any other sightings, will you please let us know?" I asked.

"Sure thing, I'm sick of worrying about it. The missus is driving me crazy, I'm not allowed to let these little'uns outta my sight. A fella can't get any rest," he replied, laughing as the tiny hatchlings swam figure of eights around him, banging headfirst into his shell without a care in the world.

"Dude, you gotta let them run free, let them make some mistakes ay. How will they ever learn otherwise?" questioned Eddie.

"You try telling the wife that," said Samson.

"Remind me never to get married," answered Eddie chuckling, "Take it easy yeah dude. Don't let those little guys get the better of ya."

We watched as Samson swam off underwater with his kamikaze bunch of tiny turtles following closely behind. Every now and then, one would zoom in front of another one. I could have stayed and watched them forever - the thought of those precious creatures being in any kind of trouble was too much to bear.

"Thanks Eddie, Samson was really cool," I told Eddie. "So do you really believe there's something to this Ocean Monster sighting?" I asked him.

"Look, I know it sounds farfetched, but I don't see why it's so unbelievable," he replied. "All I know is that something or someone is hurting a lot of animals and fish that I care about. I've surfed these waves since I was a nipper and I've never seen so much illness and death, and this is just the tip of the iceberg. Last week alone, Ryan died and just days later nine birds were found washed up dead on the beach. No one even mentioned them and we have no idea what killed them. I know that there's not much to go on but if it was up to me, I'd be mounting a proper search team to patrol the beach and find out what's going on."

"Well, have you said anything to Katia or the others?" I asked him, completely certain that Katia would be able to get to the bottom of this, if anyone could.

"I told you, they think I'm just a surfer dude and that I have a wild imagination. I'm not taking this to Katia, she's got way bigger problems to deal with and would probably just brush me off."

"I don't think she would you know, after all it's her job to protect all creatures great and small. If there's actually a

71

problem, she will want to know about it for sure," I replied, certain that I was right.

"Are you guys coming in now or hanging out for a bit? I think I'll head back," I said to Jet and Eddie. I didn't feel much like surfing anymore, the water felt really cold and I had shivers running through me. I was reminded of my dream, of being trapped underwater with a black blob reaching out threatening to swallow me up. I shuddered and wrapped my wings around myself for warmth.

"Just a few more waves, then we'll head back," answered Jet.

"Cool, catch you guys later," I shouted as I grabbed my board and flew off across the sea.

Once I was back in my room, I thought about everything I'd learned so far. Logic said that there was probably no such thing as the Ocean Monster, but if there wasn't, then what was killing all these beautiful creatures? Something sinister was going on, that was for sure. I knew that death is natural in some cases, but this many deaths and so quickly... well, that didn't seem too natural to me. One thing I did agree with Eddie on, was that right now we didn't have much to go on.

What I knew so far:

- Ryan died from an unexplained illness — his sister Milly blamed it on the Ocean Monster for some reason I didn't yet know..
- Samson the turtle also had friends who had died — they got an unexplained floating disease after they saw/felt the Ocean Monster.
- There were unexplained deaths of large numbers of birds.
- I had some weird dreams of a black blob that I was powerless to escape from.

- I heard the myths and rumours about the Ocean Monster. Were they stories told to the young to scare them, or were they based on ancient facts?

As you can see, it wasn't much to go on. I needed more information and I needed help getting it. I wondered who would be willing to help me. I was pretty certain that I could count on Eddie and Jet, and I was sure that Allie could be persuaded, so I just needed to work on Paige, Eva and Banjo. I would leave Katia out of it until we had more proof. At that point, she could officially investigate and send out a team of Protector Fairies. I knew I'd need a lot more evidence though before getting Katia involved. But a task force set up by me in secret, well... no one could stop me from doing that.

Later that night in my dreams, I was trapped deep underwater again. I struggled to break free from whatever chains or ropes were binding me, but it was no use. Samson and his tiny turtles swam around me in distress. Samson was crying out for help, but no sounds were leaving his mouth. I watched, powerless to help as his babies were snatched and engulfed in the black blob that was spreading across the seabed. It shifted and swirled - long spindly dark tentacles reaching out and grabbing each turtle in its grip before swallowing it up whole. I had never felt so helpless - none of my powers were working - and even though I knew it was just a dream, I couldn't wake myself up. The words 'You cannot fight it alone' cut through the silence. I held my breath, hoping that whoever had spoken would say something else. Then there it was again... 'You cannot fight it alone.'

And then I was back in my bedroom. I sat bolt upright.
I cannot fight what alone? That was the million-dollar question.

So now I knew that my dreams meant something, I was sure of that one thing. My gut was usually right and my gut was telling me that something was very wrong in Byron Bay. If I was to be any kind of Protector Fairy, surely I had to follow my instincts? I decided that would assemble an investigation team and we would get to the bottom of things.

I would not be alone.

TOP SECRET MISSION

I started planning immediately. If we were going to get to the bottom of this mystery and prove it to the whole Water Fairy community, we'd have to gather some real hard evidence. Everyone believed that the Ocean Monster was just a myth, so convincing them that they were wrong would not be an easy task.

I headed out at dusk to meet with my task force. Only friends that I knew I could trust had been selected and they all waited under the dancing tree, chattering amongst themselves as I arrived. To my utter disbelief, I saw that Allie had brought Sasha along too!! What was she doing? I told her that it was a secret mission. Bah! Oh well, there was not much that I could do about it... so I smiled at her whilst trying to ignore my inner feelings – really I had no idea why I'd taken such a disliking to her.

"Thanks for coming everyone," I said, addressing everyone BUT Sasha in my mind.

"As most of you know, there have been some strange deaths and illnesses lately - most recently, the terrible loss of the young dolphin Ryan from the sickness that also affected his brother Dylan. There have also been accounts of seabirds washed up dead on the shore, schools of dead fish and we just heard about a family of sea turtles as well," I explained gravely. "What's weird about all of these deaths are the circumstances surrounding them. All of the creatures were still pretty young, and none of them died of natural causes. In fact, many of them appeared healthy before suddenly being brought down by a mysterious illness. But the real reason that we're here tonight is to discuss whether the Ocean Monster could be behind these deaths," I added breathlessly.

"What makes you say that?" asked Sasha. "You only just heard about the Ocean Monster the other day and now what, you're some kind of expert are you?"

"No of course not," I snapped, "but there have been stories. I just so happen to have stumbled upon them and I think they deserve investigating... you're welcome to leave if you don't want to hear about it!" I went red in the face as I silently willed her to go away.

Sasha just huffed and stayed exactly where she was. "Okay, so let's say that we do believe you, and I for one am not saying that I do...but if we did, what stories have you heard?" she asked, staring at me indignantly.

Thankfully Eddie jumped in, and he told everyone what his friend Samson the turtle had recounted earlier that day. I watched intently as one by one they grew more concerned, especially when he told them about the poor turtles starving to death and gasping for air. Then he told them about the dead birds and numerous fish that had washed up lifeless on shore. I could tell that they were starting to take it seriously. Even Sasha had stopped objecting and just looked mildly annoyed.

"So, what you're saying is that you think there's a link between all these deaths and the Ocean Monster?" asked Allie.

"What I'm saying is that I think it deserves investigating at the very least, don't you?" I stated more than asked. "I've been having really strange dreams too," I said quietly, mainly to Allie and Jet.

"What dreams? You haven't mentioned those before," said Jet.

Reluctantly I began to fill everyone in on my dreams, about how an ominous black blob had engulfed everything living in the ocean and how powerless I felt to stop it. "I know it's only a dream, but last night I heard a voice, and it spoke to me really clearly."

"What did it say?" asked Paige.

"It said, 'you cannot fight it alone,'" I answered dramatically.

"You really expect us to believe that?" asked Sasha rolling her eyes. "Come on Allie, let's go. She's such a drama queen, and I don't know why you can't see through her. She just wants attention," said Sasha spitefully.

Thankfully Allie jumped to my defence. "Hey that's not nice. LOLA is my best friend, and if she thinks there's something worth investigating, then I believe her. You weren't there last year. You didn't see what she did to save our hometown and to save me! If LOLA thinks we should investigate, then you should all pay attention," said Allie as she moved to stand by my side. I squeezed her hand tightly and thanked her silently.

"Suit yourself then, stay and play stupid detectives, I've got better ways to spend my time," said Sasha as she waltzed off with her head high in the air.

"Why did you bring her? She's awful," I whispered to Allie.

"Sorry, I thought she was a bit of fun. She likes playing dress up and designing stuff with me, but I honestly didn't know she'd be so mean," replied Allie.

"That's okay, thanks for sticking up for me," I grinned at her.

"Always," she replied and she gave me a wink.

"Okay, enough sappy stuff, what's the plan LOLA?" said Jet, reminding me what we were there for.

"Well, I thought that we could start by conducting some interviews. We could take it in turns to head out and see who we come across. If we go in pairs, we'll cover more ground. We should start at Lennox Heads and make our way across to Brunswick Heads. That's a lot of ocean to cover, so what do you think?" I asked them all expectantly.

"What are we looking for?" asked Eva.

"Well, anything unusual really. Any unexplained deaths or strange illnesses. Especially, any stories that mention an Ocean God or any kind of Ocean Monster," I replied.

"Okay, that shouldn't be too hard," replied Eva.

"What do we say if anyone asks us why we're asking?" asked Eddie.

"Good question," I replied, thinking long and hard about my answer. "You could say that it's a school project. No one will question you if they think a teacher is behind it," I suggested.

"Okay, so when do we go?" asked Allie.

"There's no time like the present, right?" I replied, hoping that I had convinced everyone to take part.

"Why the rush?"

"Jet and I are supposed to leave for Protector Training Camp in four days so it's now or never. Plus, what if there is an Ocean Monster and more creatures are going to die? Surely if we gather enough evidence before we go to camp, we can get the real Protectors involved and then they can fight the Monster."

They all nodded in agreement.

We split into pairs. I partnered with Allie, and I felt so happy to be reunited once more with my best friend - even after her momentary lapse in judgement. Jet partnered with Eddie, of course, Eva with Paige and Banjo was left without a partner so I asked him to join our team. I began handing out my instructions - luckily I had prepared a list of places to go and questions to ask. I had maps and detailed instructions for each member of the task force to take with them.

Instructions for the Mission - Day One

Stop at four of the locations marked on your map and speak to whomever you bump into: fish, birds, dolphins, whales and even crabs if they will talk to you.

Ask the following questions...

1. Have you or anyone you care about felt ill lately?
2. Has anyone you care about died unexpectedly - and if so - do you know the cause?
3. Have you ever seen, or heard of anyone who has seen, the Ocean Monster?
4. Do you believe in the Ocean Monster?
5. Do you feel safe in the water?

When I was certain that everyone was clear on the rules, Allie and I set off towards Lennox Heads with Banjo happily buzzing behind us. Jet and Eddie headed out to Brunswick

Heads to start their investigations and Paige and Eva stayed behind to interview the locals.

As we flew, I focused my thoughts on poor Ryan and all the other beautiful creatures that had died. We owed it to them to understand what had caused their deaths and to stop it from happening again. I projected those thoughts out into the world in the hope that my fellow fairies would pick it up and it would keep everyone focused on our mission.

We came to rest at Brunswick Heads Nature Reserve. I checked my map and sure enough, it matched the scene in front of us - a beautiful sweeping curved coastline joining the river and surrounded by thick bushland. It was the perfect place to start, because the local area was bound to be teeming with wildlife.

"So do you need me to whip up a verse or two?" asked Banjo in all seriousness. "It might be heavy going you know, what with all the talk of sickness and the dreaded 'D' word. I could lighten the mood with my slick rhymes," he offered.

"Thanks, Banjo, but maybe another time," I told him, not sure what an impromptu rap would add to the situation. Don't get me wrong, I loved Banjo dearly, but he had a funny habit of saying the most inappropriate things at the worst possible times. Like that one time when Katia was hosting a posh dinner party for some fancy city-dwelling fairies and he gave a table-top wobbling performance of "I'm too sexy for my wings"... I still giggle at the memory. Needless to say, he wasn't asked to perform at any other posh dinners.

"Okay I hear you," he answered good naturedly. "If things are getting too depressing, I'll be ready though, never fear..." I didn't have the heart to tell him 'no', so I just smiled and patted his soft head.

"Let's go and find someone to interview, shall we?" I said, not quite sure where to start but hoping that some willing participants would appear. We didn't have to go far. Allie spotted a school of Humpback whales breaching in the distance. She pointed to them excitedly and we sped over to them as quickly as we could. They were quite a way out to sea and we didn't want to miss this opportunity because frankly Humpback whales are awesome!!

Reasons Why Humpback Whales Are Awesome:

1 – Just like acrobats, they can jump completely out of the water, and that's pretty impressive considering they can weigh up to 40 tons! *Dear reader, a car weighs two tons so that's like, 20 cars jumping out of the sea.*
2 – They are awesome singers and each population sings a song that is completely unique to them.
3 – They are super smart and communicate with their own special dialects.
4 – Each whale has a unique design on its belly, like a human fingerprint.
5 – They have not only one, but two blow holes, and they have to think about breathing. If they want to sleep, they turn off just half their brain and the other half stays awake so that they remember to breathe... cool huh?

I was pretty excited about meeting the whales. I'd never actually had a one-on-one conversation with a pod of whales before - you could say that I was more of a long-distance admirer of their work. I flew towards them as fast as my little wings would take me with Allie and Banjo desperately trying to keep up. We stopped smack bang in their path, just as the largest female came up through the waves and blew out a huge stream of air and water through one of her enormous blowholes. All three of us were caught up in its sheer force. It hit us directly from below and flung us into the air amidst a plume of water. Allie screamed in fright and Banjo buzzed and sputtered like he was being drowned. I acted quickly and created a force field around us, thankful that I still remembered how to do it. As the water jet died down we drifted back to the waves, tucked safely inside our force field. I noticed that the whales had stopped dead in their tracks and

were staring up at us. I suddenly got flustered and felt the
need to explain ourselves, just in case they mistook us for food
- after all, I'd never met a whale before, perhaps we looked like
a mid-afternoon snack to them?

"Hi there, long-time fan, first-time caller," I said awkwardly,
having NO idea where those words came from. I think I'd
heard it on a human T.V. show once when I was spying on
some humans. Regardless, even I knew that it was a weird
thing to say... I tried again.

"Sorry, I'm not sure what the etiquette is when one meets a
whale?" I said. Oh no, now I sounded like I was meeting the
Queen!! What does 'one' think of this, your Majesty? Really
LOLA, get a grip...

"Hello normally works," said the largest of the four whales
currently grinning up at us. Her voice was deep and booming,
and I could just imagine how beautiful her singing voice would
be.

"Yeah, or 'stoked to meet you,' that works too," said the
smallest one who had a huge white stripe down his left side
and a lazy grin on his face.

"Sorry, let's try that again. As you can see I'm a bit nervous,
I've never talked to a real-live whale before," I stuttered,
finally managing to get control of my nerves. I tried again,
determined to make a better impression this time. "Actually
we have important business to discuss with you, if that's
okay?" I said in my most grown-up voice.

"Yes, are you in any danger right now?" asked Banjo
buzzing up and down - keen to get in on the investigation. That
wasn't exactly how I would have put it, but I couldn't fault his
enthusiasm.

"Sorry to interrupt, but perhaps we should introduce
ourselves first?" suggested Allie quite wisely.

"Sorry, of course, how rude of me," I stuttered, utterly
embarrassed by my lack of manners. Thank goodness that one
of us was level headed today! I was a mess. "I am LOLA, this is
my best friend Allie and this is Banjo. We live in Byron Bay

and we are conducting a very important health and safety questionnaire."

"Well okay then. I am Matilda, this is Bruno and these two are Tully and Rodney," answered Matilda. "What did your friend mean about danger? Should I be worried? We migrate this way every year... is there something I should know about?" asked Matilda.

"No, no nothing like that," Allie assured her.

"We just have a few questions to ask if that's okay?" I said, keen to establish myself as an authority again after my embarrassing behaviour earlier.

"It's all very straight-forward I assure you," I added, holding up my questions and attaching them to a clipboard along with a pen I had hidden in my backpack.

Dear reader, have you ever noticed how much easier it is to look official if you have a clipboard and a pen?

"Fire away then," said Matilda. By now, all four of them were giving us their full attention with their heads held high out of the water, clearly quite fascinated by us. I had a feeling that they hadn't met many fairies before either. It was mutual fascination at first sight.

"Question number one..." I said in my most professional voice.

I rattled through all the questions, receiving nothing but blank expressions and negative responses. Then right at the very end when I thought it was all over, the smallest whale, who was called Tully, said something that got my attention.

"Sorry, can you say that again please?" I asked her, leaning in to make sure I had heard her orrectly.

"Ambu keeps us safe," she repeated softly.

"Ah, she means the Mermaid Ambu," said Matilda. "She loves Ambu. She met her only once, and now it's all Ambu this and Ambu that. I tell you, it's quite something to live up to."

"Sorry, what do you mean? Who's Ambu?" I asked, turning to look at Allie and Banjo to see if they had any idea who this Ambu character was. Their faces told me that they had no idea either.

"What, you mean you've never heard of Ambu? Well I never, she's only the ruler of these very waves, the Goddess of the Seas, the Queen of the Ocean. No, not ringing a bell? She's a Mermaid, like the top Mermaid I suppose you could call her!" said Matilda. "I'd have thought that all you magical creatures would be well acquainted."

I was speechless. A Mermaid, well, I wasn't expecting that.

"But, they died out years ago, I thought..." said Allie looking at me for confirmation.

"Yes, that's what I thought too," I said. "Are you sure Tully isn't confused?" I asked, quite sure that if Mermaids did still live in the oceans then surely Katia would have mentioned them at some stage.

"No I'm quite sure, thank you. My daughter knows what's what. She might be young, but she knows what's real and what isn't. Besides I've met Ambu myself, quite a day that was I can tell you!"

I apologised, angry at myself for doing to Tully exactly what I hated being done to me - assuming that just because I was young, I didn't know the difference between real and make-believe.

"So where does she live, this Ambu? How can we meet her?" I asked.

"It depends on how far underwater you can swim, because Mermaids live on the ocean floor. There's an entire Mermaid city down there ruled by Ambu, but she very rarely comes up to the surface... you'd have to go to her."

"What else do you know about her, and do you know if she has heard of the Ocean Monster? Maybe she will be able to answer our questions."

"I thought it was just a questionnaire for school..." said Matilda, wisely picking up on the eagerness of my voice. "You sound mighty anxious about this health and safety project, as you call it. Is there a danger that I should know about?"

So we filled Matilda in on everything that we knew. I figured that the more information we gave her, the more likely she would be to tell us something useful. Maybe she could even help out by taking us to see Ambu. Surely a Mermaid would know everything there is to know about the ocean she lived in.

"Thinking about it, there was a disappearance recently, but I didn't think to connect it. Nothing has happened, well nothing that we know of, but..." said Matilda thoughtfully.

Rodney started splashing and vocalising wildly. "Mum, is Blue in danger?"

"It's alright son, calm down. Yes I know he is your friend... don't start thinking the worst, I just mentioned it as it was fairly recent, and I honestly thought we'd have had word by now..." she rubbed up against him to calm him down.

Matilda told us all about an older whale called Blue that had become a good friend to her son. He looked up to him on account of all the migrations he'd done, the things he'd seen and the places he'd been. Rodney loved to listen to his songs and try and copy them. They were as thick as thieves apparently. Anyway, a couple of weeks ago, Blue just didn't turn up one day. They didn't think much of it, and Matilda thought he'd probably gone back to his own family, but Rodney was certain that something must have happened. It certainly wasn't much to go on, but I said we'd investigate anyway. Poor Rodney pleaded with his eyes and I promised him that if we could find his friend, we would. I made them tell me where they had seen Blue last and I marked the spot on my map. I was also careful to make a note of everything Matilda had said about Ambu and where to find the Mermaid City - that was definitely worth investigating!!

We said our farewells. Matilda promised that they would stick close to the coastline as they continued their migration, and that way we'd know where to find them if we got any news.

We'd spent so long with the whales that we didn't have much time left for the rest of our investigation. The sun was going down so we split up - determined to find three more interview subjects to squeeze in before it got too dark. I found a busy rockpool nearby and went to work interviewing a rather lively crab called Clive, who had a lot to say about the state of rockpools and how they were too hot to live in by far. Allie interviewed a craggy old eastern osprey who had a lot to say about the tastiness of fish in general, and how "they all tasted funny nowadays." Banjo got the lowdown from a dragonfly called Zip who didn't have much to say as it turns out, but oh my, was he pretty!

All in all, we flew back home feeling like we'd had a pretty constructive day. So what had we learned I hear you ask? You all know the drill by now...what we needed was a list.

Things We Had Learned On Our Very Important Mission!

1 - Mermaids still exist.

2 - Not only do Mermaids *exist,* but apparently there is a Mermaid city close by and it has a ruler who goes by the name Ambu.

3 - A whale called Blue has gone missing - *could it be linked to this case??*

4 - Rockpools are overcrowded and too hot to live in by far— *according to some.*

5 - Fish tastes funny- *according to some.*

6 - Dragonflies are awesome and very pretty to look at — *according to everyone.*

7 - Whales have good singing voices — *and that's just a plain fact.*

NINE

WHO IS AMBU?

Once everyone had returned to the dancing tree, which was our agreed upon meeting place, I called the meeting to order.

"Friends, fellow investigators, please gather round. I'm excited to tell you everything that we learned today, but I'm even more excited to hear what everyone else learned. Who would like to start?"

Banjo buzzed excitedly, raising his hands and bouncing up and down like a jumping bean, "Oooh pick me, pick me."

"Actually Banjo, I was hoping that someone else might start this evening, I already know what we found out," I told him laughing. His enthusiasm is just one of the many reasons why I love him so.

"Boys, why don't you start? You went to Lennox Heads, what did you find out there?" I asked Jet and Eddie.

"It's not great I'm afraid," said Eddie solemnly. "We went to Seven Mile Beach and talked to a school of salmon swimming a few miles out. They told us that they've been losing friends to weird illnesses for months now and they didn't know why. Their friends started off just feeling a bit crook and they couldn't eat, but then very quickly they went downhill. They've lost ten fish from their school alone in the past two weeks, and the salmon we spoke to reckons that someone is poisoning them," said Eddie, his eyes widening in alarm. "Who do ya reckon would want to poison fish ay?"

"I don't know Eddie, but that's what WE are going to find out!" I said, more determined than ever to get to the bottom of things.

Jet continued telling us the stories they'd heard from a lobster, two flathead and some seagulls. We listened closely to stories of mysterious disappearances, widespread illness with no explanations and a general fear that was spreading through the ocean.

However, the story that really jumped out at me was one that Paige told about a dolphin that spent two terrifying nights trapped far out at sea.

"His name is Mikey and he is a Bottlenose dolphin. He said he was heading into deeper waters to feed when he was distracted by a strange grinding noise in the distance. It didn't sound like a call he knew, and he couldn't place whether it was a whale or a dolphin so he swam deeper to investigate. Now this is where it gets weird," Paige warned us. We held our breath, waiting for her next words. "He said he saw what can only be described as an underwater graveyard filled with the bodies of whales and dolphins long since deceased. It was a tangled mess of bones surrounded by a black blob that was covering the ocean floor and obscuring his view - but he was sure he could see at least one whale struggling to break free. This is where the eerie sounds were coming from. He swam closer to investigate, but something grabbed him from behind and he was powerless to escape. Whatever it was, it cut into his flesh and held him completely bound - the more he fought, the more he was injured. He said he had never felt so scared or so helpless in his life!!"

I gasped, because this sounded EXACTLY like my dream.

"Eventually, after hours of struggling and calling out for help, he somehow managed to get free. Whatever it was loosened its grip and somehow he got away unharmed," she finished.

"Thanks goodness he wasn't hurt," I exclaimed. "Did he get a good look at it? What about the noises, did he manage to see who was making them?" I asked, hoping for any extra details that might help us unravel the mystery.

"No, he was pretty embarrassed to tell us about it. He said he was so scared that he swam away and didn't look back. He felt terrible about leaving afterwards, because he was sure that there were others left behind trying to escape. He was just too scared to go back," finished Paige.

Well, this changed everything. I was now absolutely certain that something dark and ominous was taking over the ocean.

I told the rest of the group about our encounters in Brunswick Heads and in particular about the *supposed* Mermaid - Ruler of the Ocean called Ambu. Everybody agreed that things were getting weirder and weirder by the minute and that tomorrow we should go in search of Ambu. No one had ever heard of Ambu or indeed ANY Mermaids at all! Which struck me as quite strange. Surely Water Fairies and Mermaids would know each other? I decided that it was now time to take everything we had discovered to Katia.

It was dinnertime by the time we got home and the cave was a hive of activity. We decided that it would be best to talk to Katia later that evening when everyone had gone to bed. We ate our dinner in silence trying not to let our thoughts and fears travel throughout the room. Guarding your thoughts is one of the most important things to learn as a fairy, but it was a skill I still struggled with. I can hardly manage to keep my thoughts from blurting out of my mouth at the best of times, but now I also had to control my very private thoughts - it is a LOT to manage, I can tell you.

Eventually, the main cave emptied. Katia had been entertaining a group of kids with some bedtime stories, and they finally fell asleep. Their grateful parents swooped in to pick them up and take them home to bed.

"Okay, you've all waited so patiently, now please tell me what's going on," asked Katia, picking up on everyone's nervous mood.

"We wanted to ensure that we had privacy Katia, because we have something big to share with you and we don't want to alarm anyone," said Paige.

"Okay, we have privacy now, please tell me," she urged, motioning for us all to be seated.

Paige told Katia about the dolphin called Mikey and how he had been attacked and trapped by something sinister. Then Jet jumped in to tell her about the disappearing salmon - who were dying from symptoms similar to those experienced by Ryan and Dylan, the sons of Delphine. Finally, Eddie recounted everything he had heard from Samson the turtle.

Katia looked confused, so I decided to let her in on my train of thought. I could see how all these things, whilst horrible, might not seem connected at first. I was certain, however, that once I explained my thinking and laid out the evidence in front of her, then it would all make more sense.

I explained what had led us to investigate the Ocean Monster in the first place. I reminded her of how the death of Ryan had affected me, and why I needed to understand what had caused it. Then I told her about Eva's storytelling group where I had heard the myth of the Ocean Monster (the same monster that Milly had said was to blame for her brother's death!) and how those old stories had got my imagination working overtime. I explained that the creatures we had spoken to - whether it was the turtles or the dolphins or the whales - ALL had something terrible to tell us, and that the more we investigated, the more evidence we found. Lastly, I told her about the dreams I'd been having - about a menacing black blob eating anything it came into contact with - how scary it was, and how powerless it had made me feel. So when Paige told me what Mikey the dolphin had experienced, I just knew there had to be a link. Somehow, I had dreamed that exact same thing, now how could that be?

"Well, I can certainly see that you've all been busy..." said Katia thoughtfully.

"It started out as an interesting project, and to be honest, none of us was entirely convinced, but LOLA was so passionate about it and we thought what harm could it do?" explained Paige.

"Yes, but very quickly we knew that something wasn't quite right," said Allie smiling at me, "and LOLA does have a knack for sniffing out this sort of thing."

"For the record, I never doubted LOLA for a minute," said Banjo loudly, keen to earn some brownie points.

"Okay, so let's get this straight. You started off investigating whether there is a *real* Ocean Monster, am I right?" asked Katia.

Seven heads nodded back at her in unison.

"Then you split up and interviewed some birds and marine life and found out that there have been a number of unexplained illnesses and deaths recently," continued Katia.

91

Again seven heads nodded back at her.

"Finally, LOLA you think you have somehow either had a premonition in your dreams OR you felt something similar to what a dolphin called Mikey experienced out in the deep ocean while you were lying in your bed?" finished Katia.

"Yes, but I don't know which. All I know is that in my dreams, it was exactly as he described it in real life - except that I was the one who was trapped."

"Hmmm curious indeed, you were right to bring this to me," replied Katia. " Do you have any idea why all this is happening?" she asked.

"No, that's what we thought you might be able to help us find out," I replied hopefully.

"Oh, you forgot about Ambu," said Eva quite rightly.

"Pardon?!" said Katia suddenly alert.

"Ah, of course. Yes, Ambu! How could I have forgotten," I chastised myself. "So we also found out that apparently there's a Goddess of the Oceans, and her name is Ambu. She's a Mermaid. Do you know about her? If so, how come you've never told us about her?" I asked innocently.

"Because she's not an issue. You don't need to worry about her," replied Katia quite crossly.

"So you DO KNOW about her and she really IS a MERMAID??" I repeated, quite shocked by her short reply. Surely a MERMAID was big news. It was to me anyway. The rest of the group looked equally stunned. At least I wasn't the only one in the dark for once!

"I don't like to talk about her. We haven't had reason to speak for centuries and I rather hope it stays that way," said Katia abruptly.

"But she could have important information that we need," I reasoned, not quite sure why Katia was acting so out of character.

"I'm afraid she wouldn't tell us even if she did. She's not a very nice Mermaid you see," said Katia as if that explained everything. "Your time would be better spent working out the cause of the illnesses and then we can find a cure. Plus you're off to Protector Training Camp in a few days LOLA, and you too Jet, so perhaps you should both be focusing on getting ready for that?" she said. "Why don't you leave this with me and I'll get to the bottom of it."

I was stunned, because I'd never seen Katia shut something down so quickly before. Talking about Ambu had definitely hit a nerve, there was no doubt about it but I sensed that it was best to hold my tongue. I respected Katia and admired her, so I was sure that she had her reasons for being so secretive. BUT of course, now I was even more intrigued. If someone tells me not to eat the cake, all I can think about is eating the cake! I had to find out what was going on for myself.

"Well that's that then," said Allie, after Katia bid us goodnight and told us to get some rest.

"What do you mean that's that?" I asked incredulously. "That is the worst cop-out I've ever heard."

"I know, but if Katia says to leave it alone, then what can we do? You heard her, it doesn't sound like Ambu will want to talk to us anyway and I think she sounds scary."

I realised that Allie was frightened. I didn't want to pressure her; that was the last thing I wanted to do.

"It's okay Allie, you don't have to come if you don't want to. I completely understand." I remembered everything that Allie went through last summer - being captured by the King and all – she had every right to be cautious.

"You're right about one thing Allie, it certainly doesn't sound like she's going to open her doors to us and invite us in for tea... BUT, I have to try," I said, and I looked around at my friend's faces to see who was with me.

"Count me in LOLA, we've got three more days before training camp, I've got nothing else to do," said Jet.

"I'm in," said Eddie moving to stand by his friend.

"Abso-dupely-in-fo-shizz!" said Banjo.

"Oh LOLA, go on then, I'm in too," said Paige sighing.

"Me too," added Eva.

We all waited to hear what Allie would say.

"I don't think so LOLA," she said softly, "not this time..."

I have to admit that I was disappointed, but I also understood. My friend had been through a lot and I had no idea how it must have felt to be locked up in a dungeon.

"It's okay Allie, we understand, don't we guys?" I smiled encouragingly at her.

"Sure, of course, no sweat," they all said, shrugging it off as no big deal.

I could tell that it was hard for her to say no to me. Sometimes it's harder to say no to your best friend than to anyone else.

"Okay, so I suggest that we meet again tomorrow before dawn. I think the first thing we should do is try and find Ambu, then let's get to the bottom of what she knows. If she is the Goddess of the Ocean, then surely she will know what is making everyone so sick. She might not be very friendly like Katia said, but she's bound to be concerned about what's going on!" I said, confident that OF COURSE she'd care about the ocean if she was, in fact, a *Goddess*. Protecting the ocean would likely be her number one priority. Anyway, there was only one way to find out and that's exactly what I intended to do.

I didn't sleep very well that night. I tossed and turned restlessly and kept waking up gasping for air. My thoughts were confused and my mind churned with endless chatter and dark feelings of despair. Eventually, I gave up trying to sleep and headed to the top of the cave to peer out to the ocean. The view from the top floor was amazing, you could see as far as the lighthouse and way out to sea.

"What the...?" I quickly blinked, opening and closing my eyes a few times repeatedly to check that I was seeing clearly.

The beach was a mess. It looked like someone had come along and emptied the garbage bins right onto the sand. The sea was extremely angry, the skies were dark and stormy and I could hear the turbulent wind whistling around our cave. I stood mesmerised by what I saw in front of me. Where had all this trash come from? I wondered. The beach cleanup team would have their hands full today that was for sure.

It was far too early to be up so I had decided to go back to bed when I saw a fairy flying up the beach. I squinted to see who it was when she turned around and seemed to look directly at me.

It was Katia.

She had obviously seen or heard the storm herself and gone out to investigate. But why was she out there on her own in the middle of the night? Something told me to stay hidden and keep my thoughts to myself. And then she sped off. I watched as she flew out across the waves at an alarming speed. I made a quick decision and followed her out into the night. I caught a glimmer of her as she dove under the waves, which all crashed around her with almighty force. There was nothing else for it, I had to follow her in - wherever she was going, she was going there quickly and that meant one thing... trouble.

The roar of the ocean was deafening. I flew across it, skimming the surface and desperately looking for any sign below of Katia. Eventually, I spotted her and flew as fast as I could, eager to catch her. I knew I would be slower under water (I don't have the same swimming skills as Katia or the other Water Fairies!), so I stayed just above the waves until I was directly on top of her and could confirm she wasn't moving anymore. I looked around and saw that we were miles out to sea, way farther out than I had ever ventured before. I had been so focused on chasing Katia that I hadn't been paying attention at all, I had no idea where we were. I felt frightened and alone in the vast ocean, just like in my dream.

As I peered down into the water, I saw what appeared to be a large golden dome rising majestically out of the depths. I watched on in wonder as the roof of the dome opened, like the tight bud of a flower blooming under the rays of the sun, and I saw Katia swim inside. Determined to get a better look, I dove headfirst into the ocean, fighting against the strong tides. I forced myself to swim down as far as I could, because wherever Katia was going, I wanted to go too. By the time I reached the roof of the dome, however, it had closed again. Whatever was inside was now tightly locked and sealed away, and I could find no alternate way to get inside. The outside of the dome was smooth and cold to touch and I swam for miles across and around it, looking for an entrance or some kind of button to push. I found nothing.

All I could do was wait. So I floated in the water, hoping that someone would come and open the golden dome. I was anxious to see what was inside.

The only logical explanation was that this was where Ambu lived, I was certain of it. For, who else but a Mermaid would live in a golden dome hidden deep underneath the water so far out to sea?

But the biggest question of all was why had Katia gone to see her all alone in the middle of the night? What was the big secret?

THE SECRETS OF SISTERHOOD

I floated motionless in the water for hours. No one had entered or left the dome in all that time. I was starting to think I was seeing things, had I really seen Katia swim inside the dome? Was there even a dome at all, or was I dreaming? I banged on the shiny top again to assure myself that it was real and with the hope that someone would hear me and let me in!!

Nothing happened.

I was about to give up when I heard movement in the distance. Swimming towards me were two beautiful Mermaids, although I couldn't tell if they were Mermen instead. It was too hard to see for sure, but regardless they were beautiful and elegant with strong jaws, long flowing hair and dazzling ruby eyes that shot lasers through the water in front of them like car headlights.

I was suddenly aware of the fact that I was not invited, and technically, I was spying, so I hid inside some lilac coral and watched in fascination as they approached the top of the dome. They put their hands on top, which made the dome glow red under their fingertips. Then, hey presto, the dome opened up once again.

I waited until their sleek tails had disappeared inside the dome before swimming out from behind my hiding place and following them. As I reached the entrance, the dome started closing. This time I managed to slip inside before the golden dome became a fortress once more. I remained still, holding my breath until I was sure that no one had seen me. What would I say if someone asked me who I was or what I was doing there? I had no idea, so I decided to cross that bridge when I came to it. I looked around and saw only the smooth interior of the dome. It looked like a huge corridor where the only option seemed to be travelling downward. I started to swim towards the bottom, (assuming that there must have been a bottom, even though I couldn't see it) when suddenly the walls started turning. They rotated clockwise and water rushed from behind me, turning the corridor into a huge slip and slide. I was pulled under by the force of the water and corkscrewed down the corridor, gathering speed and being pushed from side to side as the slip and slide gained momentum.

Eventually, I was spat out onto a sandy seabed. I brushed the sand off me and stood up to take in my surroundings. The sea appeared to be deserted, and it was very dark. I had never actually seen such a dark place, it was eerie and my immediate reaction was to turn around and look up back to where I'd come from - hoping that I could get out again. Out of the corner of my eye, I saw neon lights flashing everywhere, but I couldn't work out what they were. As my eyes got used to the darkness, I became aware of hundreds of sets of eyes staring at me. Then I could hear whispers saying, "She's not from around here, that's for sure," and, "Ooh, just you wait until they find her." As I got closer and saw who was doing all the talking, I almost screamed out in fright. Oh dear, whatever these creatures they were most unpleasant to look at indeed!

"Yeah alright, calm down, no need to look so horrified," said one fish, who looked like something had eaten half of his head. "I know pretty is not my middle name," he said matter-of-factly.

"Not at all, sorry I just wasn't expecting to see you there," I said, quickly apologising, I remembered that it's not nice to judge a book (or a fish) by its cover, even if it does look half-eaten!

"Well, what did you expect to find down here? A fancy-pants Mermaid I suppose?" and he said Mermaid like this – *Merrrrmayyyd* - all snooty and posh, wiggling his fins in a mocking gesture.

"Don't you like Mermaids then?" I asked, as it seemed like he wasn't a fan.

"Well let's put it this way: How would you like to be cooped up in the deep sea with a bunch of prancing wannabes who don't do anything but whine about how wonderful everything used to be in the good old days?" he asked me.

"Well, I'm sure they're not all that bad," I said, keen to move the conversation onto something more useful, like where I could find Katia.

"Oh they are Miss Fairy, oh yes they are!" exclaimed a bright purple blob. Sorry, but there's no nice way to describe this particular creature from the deep. I was looking at a purple blob with two eyes and what appeared to be six arms or legs - I couldn't quite tell. When it opened its mouth to speak, its eyes rolled back onto the top of its head and its face became a huge black hole. These creatures were freaking me out! I was determined to remain open-minded, because they seemed friendly enough despite appearing very strange.

"Okay, so what am I dealing with here?" I asked hesitantly. "Tell me everything I need to know. I followed my friend Katia the Queen of the Water Fairies down here and I need to know if she is in any danger."

The blob just burped in response. Clearly, that was all I was getting out of it. I turned my attention back to the half-eaten head fish.

"If you mean the blonde one with wings like you, then yes she's here. I saw her going into Ambu's private caves earlier, they're over that way," he pointed to a bright light glimmering in the distance. "I wouldn't go in there if I was you though. I heard them shouting so I'm staying well clear of them. If your friend gets Ambu any more worked up, who knows what she'll do. She's already in a terrible mood, who do you think is behind that nasty storm out there!" he said shaking his head. "Now that I know she's the Queen of the Water Fairies, well, that makes a lot more sense. Ambu doesn't like her sister, I know that much," he said smugly.

"What do you mean, Sister?!? Are you saying that Ambu and Katia are related?" I asked incredulously.

"Well *sort of* - but you wouldn't know it, there's no love lost there I can tell you!"

Well, this was most unexpected!

News alert!!

1 - Katia has a *sort of* secret sister.
2 — Katia's *sort of* secret sister is a Mermaid!
3 — Katia's *sort of* secret sister, the Mermaid, is Ambu - only the Goddess of the Oceans that we've been hearing so much about!!

The half-eaten head fish and the purple blob were now watching me very closely. Clearly, I was providing them with entertainment, the like of which they had not seen for quite a while. Surrounding the ringleaders, staring at me with their big creepy eyes, was the weirdest gang of fish you have ever seen. There was a yellow and orange upside-down fish. His eyes were on his belly and he seemed to be literally swimming upside down and flapping his fins the wrong way - it was most confusing. Then there was a jellyfish that kept electrocuting itself and jolting up a few feet in shock - I mean actually electrocuting himself with his own tentacles! I would have giggled, but I imagined that it would be very annoying to electrocute yourself every five minutes and I'm sure if he could help it he surely would. Then there were other fish that resembled the half-eaten head fish - as if someone had begun feasting on them only to get bored half way through. Some of them were missing huge chunks in the middle so that I could see parts of their spine - I had no idea what was holding them together at all and they had huge teeth and terrifying grins. And, if that's not enough to boggle your minds, there were hundreds of tiny neon flickering fish that constantly changed colour. These were not scary in the slightest, but their constant flickering was quite distracting. It was like someone kept turning the Christmas tree lights on and off - can you imagine how annoying that is when you're trying to concentrate? What a strange and eerie bunch!

I considered my next move carefully. I had no idea who I could trust. After all, I had just met these fish, and they could have been bad news. But something told me that whilst they looked a little strange, they were just regular fish with a few quirks, nothing to be scared of.

"Do you know why they fell out in the first place?" I asked the half-eaten head fish (whose name, as I found out later, was Snapper - fish have a strange sense of humour it seems).

"Well before my time I'm afraid... but the rumour I heard was that it had something to do with Ambu's plans to rid the world of humans. You know world domination and all that?... apparently, Katia isn't a big fan of Ambu's plan to flood the world and reclaim it all as ocean," said Snapper.

"Oh, so just something small then, nothing to worry about!" I exclaimed in fright, sure that he was pulling my leg.

"Well, if you think the end of the world as you know it is small, then fair dues to you... frankly it makes no difference to us. The deep ocean is our home and we can hide out on the ocean floor until it all blows over. We'll be alright, but it would mean the end of the line for humans and I believe even you fairy folk would struggle to survive with no land to live on don't you think?"

"I was being sarcastic, I thought you were joking!" I said, completely lost for words.

"Oh, sorry I don't really DO sarcasm, I'm a fish," he answered as straight-faced as a half-eaten fish head could be.

"But, why does Ambu want to flood the world and why now?"

"Well, then there will be no more humans to pollute anything will there? She can clean up the ocean and make it a paradise again!" he added.

"I'm sorry, I still don't understand. What exactly has she got against humans?" I asked him.

"Really? Have you stopped to look around recently? Humans are treating the ocean like their own personal garbage heap. Did you know that there's more plastic in the sea than fish right now? I may not agree with Ambu's plan to flood the world, but I certainly agree that something needs to change!" said Snapper, angrily snapping his jaws. Bob and the rest of the bunch bobbed up and down and blew bubbles in agreement.

And then it dawned on me... Ambu must be the Ocean God, aka the Ocean Monster. Except HE was a SHE!! Maybe this was what I had been searching for. Ambu knew exactly who was poisoning the ocean and she knew who to punish... humans.

Oh no, this was not good - our job was to protect the planet and everything that lived on it, and that included humans. If humans were the cause of all the sickness and deaths then I agreed that something had to be done, but a flood was not the answer. I realised what a huge mess I'd got myself tangled up in.

"Okay I'm going in," I told the motley crew of fish.

"No, no don't be silly!" said Snapper.

"Are you crazy?" screeched Bob.

"She'll turn you into a mud crab!" said another.

I gritted my teeth and shut my ears to their protests as I swam determinedly towards the caves in search of Ambu and Katia. One way or the other, I would get to the bottom of this and we would find a solution together that didn't involve floods or any living creature being hurt.

ELEVEN

LOVE HURTS

As I approached the bright light, I knew that Katia was close by. I could hear her voice and I could feel her energy, but something wasn't quite right. A force of some kind was stopping me from getting any closer and as I tried to swim, it was like I'd hit an invisible wall. I pushed and punched and kicked at it, but I was getting nowhere. It was as if the water had turned to tar and the more I tried to swim through it, the harder it pushed back at me. Argh, this was useless! What kind of magic was this and who was stopping me from getting to Katia? I looked back at my weird fishy friends for a clue and they looked as stumped as I was. It was clear that they had never seen this before. Then a voice filled my head.

"LOLA, leave now before she sees you," it was Katia. She was trying to protect me.

"No way, I came to get you and I'm not leaving without you," I promised her using only my mind.

"LOLA, please I don't have time to explain, but you have to trust me. Ambu is planning to flood the coast to punish humans for polluting her home. You need to go back and bring help, I underestimated her rage, I thought I could get through to her but it's clear she's determined to flood the earth. She's way too strong I'm afraid, I can't stop her alone," said Katia, pleading with me to listen.

"But how will a flood change anything? All it will do is cause destruction and mayhem?" I was terrified of what might happen if I left Katia alone with Ambu.

"I know that LOLA, but my sister's not thinking clearly. She's sick of watching her friends get ill and die because of pollution and she thinks this is the only way to stop humans from causing any more damage," said Katia.

"But why has she chained you up?" I could see clearly in my mind that Katia was chained down by some kind of magic force field that was glowing red hot around her.

"Because she knows I'll do everything in my power to stop her plan, and she's right! LOLA we don't have time, you must leave now before she realises that you're here. Somehow she hasn't detected you yet, but when she does, I can't protect you. Go now and bring back help!!"

She had my attention.

But how would I get out?

I frantically swam back to where my new fishy friends were still watching me with amused interest. Clearly, they had not heard my exchange with Katia, so it must have looked odd that I was suspended in mid-air with my eyes closed for so long.

"How do I get out of here?" I asked half-eaten head fish.

"What about your friend, I thought you came down here to rescue her?" he asked.

"Never mind that, plans have changed. I have to go and get help. How do I get out?" I repeated urgently.

"Well technically, you can go back out the way you came in but the problem is that the water only runs one way, that's why we are stuck here - we can't swim up against the force of the water," he explained.

"Well I'm a fairy so I can just fly out, can't I?" I reasoned.

"Good point, so you can, oh lucky you!" said Bob the purple blob, and then he started wailing.

"What's wrong?" I asked him.

"I just wish I could leave this wretched place too!" he wailed. "I only came in here looking for some food, and I didn't realise then that I'd be trapped down here forever," he moaned, crying and blubbering to himself.

I looked around at the odd bunch of misfit fish, thinking to myself that they didn't seem to belong together at all. It was a very strange assortment indeed. I wondered how long they'd been stuck in here like this.

"So do you mean to tell me that none of you actually chose to live here, and that you're all here by mistake?" I asked them.

"Yes Missy, that's a fact. Each of us came by accident, curiosity I suppose you'd call it. But we didn't realise that we'd be stuck in here for life with Miss Temperamental over there! There's a big wide ocean out there and we just long to swim in it again instead of going round in circles inside this giant fish bowl," said Snapper.

"Well let's get moving then. I'm getting you out of here!" I said, determined to do just that. "Now grab some of that seaweed, and hold on as tightly as you can - use your teeth if you have to! I'm going to fly up the chute and pull you all up behind me okay?" I told them. They all nodded except one. The jellyfish (whose name was Sparky - I told you fish had a good sense of humour) was backing away from the group.

"You go on ahead, I'll be fine here," he said.

"But why? This may be your only chance for freedom," I urged.

"I'll sting everyone. I can't control it and I don't want to hurt you all," he said sadly.

Hmmm, I thought, he had a point. An electric shock every few minutes was not going to help us reach the top and some of the smaller fish might not survive it!

What to do?

Eureka!

"I've got it!" I shouted.

"Sparky, you will lead the way with me. I'll create a force field around us, that way when you sting, it will only be us that gets a jolt and we can handle it, everyone else will be protected. What do you think? Shall we test it out?" I asked him, keen to show everyone how it would work.

"LOLA go now, quickly!" it was Katia urging me to hurry up in my mind. Argh, I'd taken too long, there was no time for testing - we had to take our chances.

"Sorry no time for testing, you need to trust me, let's go," I said, as I created a protective force field around Sparky and myself. Using strings of seaweed as a rope, we formed a long chain and headed straight up the golden chute. I flew up as fast and as close to the edge as I could, careful to avoid the water plummeting down to the ground. I briefly glanced over my shoulder and could see a line of bobbing fish all hanging on for dear life, most of them using their teeth to cling on. As we approached the top I had a moment of panic. The golden dome was closed, how would we open it? Sparky sprang to action and reached out with his long electric blue tentacles. He placed them in the middle of the dome roof, and with one almighty shock, he zapped the roof. Miracle of all miracles, it worked! The dome opened up above us and we swam out to safety.

"Woo hoo!"

"Go Sparky!"

"Freedom at last!"

Sparky looked very happy with himself as everyone swam around him, congratulating him in excitement.

"I hate to love you and leave you, but I have somewhere I need to be," I said, remembering my mission.

"Is there anything we can do to help?" asked Sparky.

"Actually there is, can you keep watch right here whilst I go and get help?" I asked him - thinking that having a look out would be a good idea. For starters, it would be hard for me to find this exact same spot again, and secondly knowing who was coming in and out of the dome might prove useful. So far, I'd only seen two other Mermaids entering the dome, but surely there were others inside.

"Right then, you can count on us, can't she gang?" said Snapper puffing up his half-eaten chest.

"Legends! I'll be as quick as I can, I promise. Once I raise the alarm, I'll have an entire Water Fairy army with me and Mr. Holt. No one messes with them!" I said proudly.

"Be careful LOLA, you haven't come across Ambu before, she's mighty fierce when she wants to be," warned Snapper.

"I'd expect no less from any sister of Katia, but even so, there's strength in numbers and I definitely have the numbers," I answered him confidently.

I flew off in search of help.

I thought that it was a 99% certainty that (considering the huge swells that must be raging) I'd find Jet and Eddie out for their morning surf, so I decided to head there first. They could help me rally the troops. Sure enough, as I neared the familiar sight of Clarke's Beach (one of Byron's most popular surfing beaches), I spotted Jet and Eddie surfing a particularly gnarly wave. Jet looked up at me in surprise as I flew towards him and waved frantically at him to follow me. They both surfed

the wave into shore and hopped over to see what I wanted.
Only Jet could tell I was worried, Eddie didn't know me well
enough yet to read my expressions.

"LOLA, what is it?" asked Jet.

"It's Katia, she's in trouble. She's been captured by her
sister Ambu, the Goddess of the Oceans. It's a long story but if
we don't do something soon, the whole coast will be flooded," I
rushed out.

"Whoa, slow down LOLA, what do you mean?" said Jet.

"Katia has a sister, since when?" asked Eddie.

"I know right, it's a LOT to take in!" I replied. "Sorry, I'll try
and quickly break it down for you." I began explaining how the
storm had awoken me and that I'd noticed Katia out of the
corner of my eye. How she'd rushed off so suddenly that I knew
there must be trouble so I followed her. How she had
disappeared inside a mysterious golden dome that I'd snuck
into and met my new fishy friends. How I had discovered that
Katia had been captured by the Ocean God; who it turns out is
actually a *Goddess* called Ambu and Katia's long lost sister.
And finally how Ambu was plotting to flood the world and rid
it of humans and us if she has her way!!!

Phew, no wonder they look shocked, it was pretty hard for
me to wrap my head around too!

"What should we do LOLA?" asked Eddie.

"First things first, we MUST find Mr. Holt. Jet do you think
you can find him? I'll go and see Reaya - maybe she has seen
something in the future that will help us in the present," I told
him.

*Dear reader Reaya was a very gifted human I'd met last
year through Katia, and her special ability was seeing into the
future.*

"Eddie can you go and warn everyone at the cave, and make
sure they all wait for us? I'll meet you back there and we can
come up with a plan to save Katia. Okay?" I asked.

"Okay," they replied in unison.

110

We went our separate ways, each determined to fulfil our part of the mission. I just hoped that Reaya was at home. Even if we could save Katia, I still had no idea how we would stop Ambu from unleashing a flood if her mind was really set on it. From everything I'd heard, Ambu was equally as powerful and determined as Katia, so I'd hate to be in the middle of a power struggle between those two. I couldn't help but wonder what had happened to them in the past; why didn't the sisters talk anymore?

I arrived at Reaya's house to see her looking out of her window; she was clearly expecting me.

"LOLA come in, come in, it's okay, you can take a breath," said Reaya as I flew inside to rest on her kitchen table.

I took a few moments to catch my breath and then I began to tell her everything I'd learned. It wasn't long before Reaya interrupted me.

"It's okay LOLA, I know why you're here, but I'm afraid this time it's quite a murky situation and I don't have a clear answer for you," she said with regret.

"What do you mean, please tell me you know how to stop Ambu and save Katia?" I pleaded with her.

"It's not that simple I'm afraid LOLA. This is a complex problem and the only thing I can tell you is that many forces will need to work together to solve it and it can't be solved overnight," she replied cryptically.

"Okay, so who are these forces and how can I find them?" I asked her.

"The forces will be ready when you need them. Heal the bond between Ambu and Katia first and then everything else will be resolved in time," she replied.

"That might prove to be a LOT harder than it sounds. I was just there and Ambu had Katia tied up in red-hot chains!" I exclaimed. "I don't think they'll be braiding each other's hair anytime soon, do you?" I said in frustration.

"I didn't say it would be easy, all I know is that first you must heal their relationship. Trust your instincts LOLA, you can remind them of what they both love. Everything else can and will be fixed in time, trust me. Help will arrive when you need it," Reaya assured me.

"I do trust you," I said, calming down a bit. "I had just hoped I'd get a clearer set of instructions, that's all."

"Don't we all," chuckled Reaya. "If only life came with a roadmap and a clear set of instructions, it would be so easy. But if you remember what I'm saying, I promise when the time is right, it will make sense. Trust yourself LOLA and trust your gut, it's the best compass you have."

"Okay if you say so, I must admit I don't feel very confident," I told her worrying that my gut wouldn't be much help in this situation.

"You'll be fine, I have faith in you LOLA. Besides, I have a few errands to run first," she answered. I wasn't so sure that this was really the time for "errands," but I could see that she'd told me all she was going to. I had to trust that at some point, what she said would make more sense to me.

"Bye then. Wish me luck!" I said as I turned to fly back to the caves.

"Remember, the answer lies in them remembering what they love LOLA," said Reaya as she retreated back inside her house and closed her window.

"This day gets weirder by the minute," I muttered to myself.

How was I supposed to fix a relationship between two sisters, one of whom was a Water Fairy Queen and one of whom was a Mermaid? And what was with that anyway; how could one of them be a Mermaid and one of them be a Fairy with the same set of parents?

And that's when I knew what I had to do... Surely something had happened a long time ago that had broken their bond. I needed to find someone who knew them before they became estranged. I decided to make a quick detour.

I knew exactly who to talk to.

TWELVE

WHERE IT ALL BEGAN

"The trouble with Ambu and Katia," said Matilda, "is that they are both stubborn. Neither of them is willing to make the first move, so nothing changes. It's very sad actually, they were so close when they were young."

"But, you see, that's what I don't understand. Ambu is a Mermaid and Katia is a Water Fairy. How exactly are they sisters?" I asked Matilda, the beautiful whale who had told me about Ambu in the first place.

"I know it may seem strange but they were raised as sisters from a very young age and they didn't notice their differences until they got much older. Katia was found abandoned on the beach when she was just a baby by Ambu's parents who were Mermaids. They took Katia in and raised her as their own child alongside Ambu. Katia is a Water Fairy by birth so with a few special charms, she can live quite happily underwater just like the Mermaids. She may not have a tail, but in all other ways she is very much like them.

Ambu and Katia did everything together when they were younger. They played make-believe, pretending to rule the oceans and sing to the whales and the fishes in the sea. Everyone loved them and it was a very happy time for all marine life. But one stormy evening, something tragic happened. A boat full of humans got into trouble far out to sea, Katia spotted them sinking and begged her parents to save them. Now Mermaids don't normally interfere in the affairs of humans (that's not their job) but because Katia was so upset they decided to do what they could to help. So the Mermaid couple went to the humans' aid, and they never returned. The boat, the humans and Ambu and Katia's parents all vanished into thin air. Ambu blamed Katia, because she thought the humans didn't deserve her parents' help in the first place. She could never forgive Katia for sending them to their death. Katia was understandably devastated, she tortured herself with guilt and begged for the forgiveness of her sister, but Ambu turned to stone, becoming angry and cold-hearted. She cut herself off from everyone, built the Mermaid City to keep herself and her fellow Mermaids safe from harm, and banished

Katia, telling her that she was no longer welcome. Katia felt so guilty that she left without question and fled to dry land to start a new life on her own," Matilda sighed as she finished telling the sad tale.

"So do you think this is Ambu's way of getting revenge on Katia and why now?" I asked her.

"Good question, because the sisters have had a truce in place for decades. They both agreed to stay out of each other's business. Ambu seemed happy to rule the deep seas whilst Katia eventually blossomed on the land, forging a new life and earning her position as the Queen of the Water Fairies. Her power grew as did her influence and Ambu knew better than to challenge a Water Fairy of such strength and who was so beloved by all creatures. But secretly she festered, growing jealous of Katia and wishing for her downfall – she never forgave Katia for the death of her parents. Now that she can prove the harm that humans are doing to the ocean, she has the perfect excuse to have her revenge. She is intent on reclaiming the earth as ocean and wiping out humans for good."

"So how are we supposed to fix this? Ambu is right in one aspect. From what I've seen, the oceans are sick and it is the humans' fault," I replied, finally understanding what Reaya had said. This was a complex issue indeed.

"Well that's the million-dollar question isn't it?" said Matilda.

"Reaya thinks we need to fix their relationship and that the rest will happen in time. Do you understand what she means by that?" I asked.

"I think that sounds very wise. Ambu and Katia are more alike than they are different. You can remind them of their similarities and remind them of the good times they shared. Then they can work together on a solution, hopefully one that doesn't involve lots of humans and innocent creatures dying!! If they would only work together, maybe the earth and the ocean has a chance of survival," said Matilda sadly.

115

"Would you please come back to the coast with me? I need to alert everyone back at the cave and I know they'll want to hear this story," I asked her.

"Of course, hop on then."

She motioned for me to grab onto her huge fin. I remembered that the last time I had been on a whale's back it had been a joyous experience. This time my mind was so completely full with worry that I hardly even noticed the beautiful scenery whizzing past and the cool air whooshing through my hair.

As we got closer to the shore, I was a bundle of nerves. The cave was full of Water Fairies anxious to know what was going on and concerned about their Queen Katia.

I hopped off Matilda's back and asked her to wait as close by as she could - she had to stay a certain distance out to sea as it was too shallow for her near the beach.

"I'll put the word out too, I have plenty of friends who have been affected by the pollution. They desperately want a solution, but even they don't want any harm to come to the humans. It will take a lot of voices to convince Ambu that there's another way to solve the issue," said Matilda.

"Thanks, I think we'll need as much help as we can get. I'll be back as quickly as I can," I promised her.

I flew across the waves, up the beach and into my home. As expected, the caves were full to the brim of concerned Water Fairies.

"LOLA, LOLA where is Katia?" they cried.

"Where is our Queen?"

"Take us to her!"

"Lead the way!"

The noise was so deafening that I could hardly think straight.

"Everyone please," I shouted as I spread my wings and rose above their heads to get their attention.

"I know you are worried, I am too, but what Katia needs now is for us to keep a cool head. We need to think clearly and form a plan to rescue her. I have spoken with Reaya."

"What did she say? Did she see us rescuing Katia?" asked Paige urgently.

"Why has Katia been captured in the first place?" asked a tall dark-haired fairy whose name I couldn't quite remember.

"I know you all have a lot of questions, but I'm afraid I don't have the time to answer them now. I have brought a whale called Matilda here to explain the full story. I need you to stay close by and be ready to help with the rescue efforts if the worst happens," I said gravely.

"What might that be?" asked one fairy.

"Yes what should we be getting ready for?" asked another.

"A flood, a flood of epic proportions, the like of which you have never seen before. If Ambu goes through with her threat, it will wipe out the coast and thousands could be killed," I replied, shivering at the very thought of it.

"What about our homes?" shouted Scotty.

"They will be washed away in the flood too, but I'm afraid that will be the least of our worries Scotty. If Ambu goes through with her plan, the earth will be reclaimed as ocean and every land-dwelling creature will be drowned," I told him.

This was met with hushed silence as the room full of Water Fairies took in the magnitude of the threat we were facing.

"What are you planning then LOLA?" asked Eva.

"First things first we need to save Katia. I'll head back to the Mermaid City now with a small group – we will free Katia and then work out our next move. Everyone else needs to stay here and be ready to protect the land if Ambu does strike; it will take a lot of protective shields to save as many humans and animals as you can. Banjo, I need you to be my eyes and ears, head to high ground and be ready to tell me anything unusual you see. If you see the seas rising or anything threatening at all, I need you to contact me okay?"

Banjo nodded furiously.

"Also I'll tell you what's going on when we get to Katia and Ambu and you will keep everyone here informed, got it?" I asked him.

"Got it LOLA, you can count on me, I won't let you down," said Banjo buzzing furiously.

"Paige and Eva, I could use your help, are you up for it?"

"Absolutely!" they said and I saw a twinkle in their eyes that I recognised. Some people come alive under pressure, and Paige and Eva had this fighting spirit. I smiled at them both, grateful to have them by my side.

"Mr. Holt, we need you of course, and please bring something that can open a locked door," I said, thinking we'd need both his super strength and clear thinking to outsmart Ambu.

"Jet and Eddie I'll leave you both in charge of setting up the protective shields across the coast. You know the beaches better than anyone here. Have a think about where would be the worst affected if the seas flood, and position everyone ready to save as many creatures as possible."

"No problem, LOLA, we can handle that no sweat," said Jet and he began organising the Water Fairies into groups, ready to deploy them across the coast.

"Who put you in charge? How come you're making all the decisions and bossing everyone around?" asked Sasha, pushing her way to the front and giving me a nasty sneer.

"Really Sasha? If it wasn't for LOLA, we wouldn't even know that Katia was missing in the first place. Besides, I don't see you having any bright ideas," said Paige jumping to my defence.

"Yeah it's called leadership, you should try it sometime," said Scotty, putting Sasha in her place.

Sasha mumbled something inaudible and shrank back into the crowd. I decided to just ignore her. She wasn't worth my energy and I had bigger things to worry about.

"What about me LOLA?" asked Allie. "How can I help?"

"I'd love you to come too Allie, but only if you're sure. It might be dangerous," I warned her.

"I understand, but I really want to help," she said, her eyes pleading with me. If Allie was ready to face whatever lay ahead, then I wasn't going to stop her. I was glad to have my best friend by my side.

"Okay let's go then," I shouted and flew out of the caves with Mr. Holt, Allie, Paige and Eva following closely behind. I wasn't sure if going head to head with Ambu was a foolish idea, but I knew we had to try. As we flew, I filled them all in on what I'd learned about Ambu and Katia being raised as sisters, how Ambu had never recovered from their parents' disappearance and how she blamed Katia and the humans for what happened. They were all shocked, and not even Mr. Holt knew that Katia had been raised with Mermaids.

As we approached the Mermaid City, I could see my unlikely bunch of fishy friends waiting at the top of the golden dome, just as I had asked them to. I quickly made the introductions. If the weird looking fish freaked my friends out, they certainly did a good job of hiding it. Unlike me, they didn't seem quite so perturbed by their half-eaten, neon flashing, electric shocking, blob-like appearances.

"Nothing too fishy to report," said Snapper cheekily.

"Although, the seas have been getting choppier and I don't like the look of those clouds," said Bob the purple blob as his eyes rotated to the top of his bulbous head.

"I noticed the weather is getting worse. Do you think Ambu is behind the storm?" I asked him.

"Hard to tell, but if it is her she's just getting started. So what's the plan? Where's your army? You mentioned something about getting an army, surely this isn't it?" asked Snapper looking very unimpressed by our small numbers.

"Change of plan again," I told him. "We need to fix the relationship between Ambu and Katia first. The army is back in Byron Bay, ready to deal with the flood if we are unsuccessful."

I was still not 100% certain of the plan myself. How I was going to make two sworn enemies friends again was quite a mystery even to me. I was putting my ultimate trust in Reaya. If she believed that this was the solution, then this was what we had to do. Somehow, someway I had to repair the bond between the sisters.

"Okay, good luck with that then," said Snapper.

"How are we going to get in, it looks completely closed," said Allie, swimming around the dome frantically looking for an entrance.

"Ah, this is where Sparky comes in. Sparky if you would do the honours please?" I asked my little blue jellyfish friend. Sparky bowed and headed towards the top of the dome, where he zapped it with all of his tentacles. It quickly burst open for us.

"Why did you ask me to bring this then?" asked Mr. Holt looking down at his wrench.

"We'll need that to get back out again," I told him. "I don't expect Sparky or the others to come back inside. They deserve their freedom, they've been trapped inside the dome for years and I couldn't possibly ask them to risk being captured again."

"Mighty nice of you Missy," said Snapper, "but if you think we're going to miss out on all this excitement, you've got another thing coming. We like to be where the action is. It isn't the fact that we were locked up that was the problem, it was the mind-numbing boredom of having nothing to do! I don't think I'm alone when I say 'sign me up,' I'm in fins and all," said Snapper again, puffing up his see-through chest in a show of strength.

"Ooh yes, I definitely want to see this," said Bob.

Sparky was already inside when he reminded us to get a move on, "Erm, I hate to point out the obvious, but perhaps you might like to get inside now?" he said. "It might look easy, but a shock of that size quite takes it out of me, and I'd prefer not to have to do it more than absolutely necessary."

"Sorry Sparky, of course, what was I thinking? Everyone follow me, but don't start heading down until we're all safely inside together. The water can take you by surprise," I warned them.

Everyone waited nervously inside the dome roof, ready to follow my lead.

"Now don't be scared, it's just like a giant water slide going down. I'll meet you at the bottom," I said as I swam forwards, waiting for the water to rush behind me and propel me downwards.

The water spat us all out onto the same seabed I had landed on before, the only difference being that this time I knew where I was and what to expect. I immediately heard the sound of Ambu and Katia arguing and I got the sense that time was running out. As one by one my friends landed with a thud next to me, I motioned for them to stay quiet. I still had no idea how we were going to distract Ambu and get Katia free from her chains.

"See this! This is the world you are trying to protect! Look at all the pain and suffering," screamed Ambu and the entire golden dome sprang to life with terrible images. It was hard to look at, there were scenes of dead fish and seabirds, dolphins cut badly by discarded fishing rope and jagged bits of plastic, fires blazing destroying precious rainforests, birds covered in oil and gasping for breath, and seas filled with trash that ended up in the bellies of innocent creatures. Ambu had created a mind movie of the damage caused by humans to the land and the ocean and was projecting the images onto the walls of the dome to torture Katia. Watching the scenes flickering around me I was shocked to see what looked exactly like the black blob from my dreams – and now that I could see it clearly I could tell that it wasn't a black blob at all – but it was made up of hundreds of pieces of discarded plastic and metal, all swelling together to form a menacing brooding shape that tangled with everything in it's path. So Ambu was NOT the Ocean Monster after all! She was NOT the cause of all the deaths and illnesses. The pollution was the real enemy!

"But you think that by flooding the land and causing even more destruction that things will get better?" asked Katia. "What kind of twisted logic is that?" she cried.

"It's the only way to save the ocean, because if there are no more humans, there will be no more pollution!" shouted Ambu. "It's too late, you've had your time Katia and you have failed! Things are worse now than they've ever been. It's time for a new way of life – one without humans!"

And with that, she rose majestically from the seabed. We watched on in horror as Ambu's head rolled back 90 degrees and she shot laser beams into the sky with her eyes, which were now glowing a brilliant red. We were pushed back as immense electric waves came off her body and pulsed through the dome. Within seconds, the previous darkness was illuminated and we could see passageways and rooms containing other Mermaids that had not been visable before. There must have been at least a dozen of them, all in the same deep trance, raising their eyes to the sky and shooting red laser beams up into the clouds.

This was our time to strike. We had to free Katia. Ambu and her followers were clearly intent on wiping out the earth. I could tell that unless we saved Katia, we had no hope of stopping them.

"Quickly this way," I said motioning to the others to follow me. We carefully avoided the Mermaids and crept over to where Katia was being held down by red-hot glowing chains.

"LOLA, Thomas, all my wonderful friends, what a welcome surprise you are," whispered Katia. "As you can see, you've caught me in quite a tight spot. A little help please?" she said shaking her chains in frustration.

Sparky set about removing her chains. They seemed to be made from some form of electricity, so he was able to interrupt the flow long enough for Mr. Holt to free Katia.

"I met with Reaya," I said, looking meaningfully at Katia. "She said we had to fix your relationship with Ambu first and then everything else would be fixed in time."

122

"That's a bit cryptic. Did she say anything else? My power crazy sister seems intent on flooding the earth. I don't know if some sister-to-sister bonding is very likely right now, what do you think?" Katia pointed over to where Ambu was still shooting laser beams out of her eyes and now was also blowing black smoke out of her mouth. Outside I could hear the seas wailing, lightening striking and thunder clapping. Goodness only knew what it was like on shore!

"Katia I know it seems impossible but Reaya has always been right in the past, so it's got to be worth a try," insisted Mr. Holt.

"I'll try, but how am I supposed to get through to her?" asked Katia, which was a fair question, because from where I was standing Ambu looked positively terrifying!

"Surely you remember *something* good about her, was she always so angry?" I asked her. To think that these two were once sisters was unimaginable - Katia was such a pure spirit she shone like a beacon of white light, and Ambu was filled with a dangerous rage that polluted the air around her. They were like night and day.

"No, she changed. She was happy once," said Katia. I could see the flicker of sadness in her eyes as she remembered how her sister once was.

"You have to remember that, Katia," I told her. "Think back to when you were both happy, and take us there. I know it sounds silly, but it is our only hope. You have to try and connect with her," I urged. I had no idea if this would actually work, but we had no other options and time was running out.

"Everyone grab Katia's hands, she is going to project her memories to us and we are going to fill the room with them, okay?"

"Okay," they replied in unison. We stepped forward to form a circle around Katia with our hands tightly clasped together. Katia began to project her childhood memories into our minds.

At first, it was blurry. It was like looking at old photographs that have been bleached with age. The scenes flickered in and out, alternating between Ambu's visions of pollution and destruction and Katia's images of their once happy childhood. Gradually, Katia's images got stronger and laughter filled the dome as we watched Katia and Ambu as young girls playing happily together - dressing up as princesses and hosting plays whilst turtles and whales watched on with glee. Soon we were able to hear entire conversations as the two young girls promised to never ever be separated and to live in matching palaces with fish and turtles and dolphins as their playmates.

Ambu was jolted out of her trance and turned to scowl at Katia, her eyes still glowing an ominous shade of red. She spewed plumes of acrid black smoke in our direction forcing us to break our circle, falling backwards while coughing and spluttering to avoid the toxic smoke.

"How did you get free?" she snarled at Katia, and then she noticed us and laughed nastily in our direction. "What are you trying to do? Do you REALLY think that you and your little friends can show me a few memories and I'll have a change of heart? It is very touching sister dearest, but we are way beyond silly sentimentalities, don't you think? Besides, you don't care about me so stop trying to pretend that you do. You left me here to rot and never looked back!"

"That is not true. I tried to get through to you, again and again, but you blamed me for our parents' death. It wasn't my fault, it was a tragic accident. I was a child too but you pushed me away. When you banished me you broke my heart!" said Katia, and I could feel her heart breaking as clearly as if it were my own heart.

Katia rose to meet her sister eye to eye. The purest rays of white light flooded from her body like sunlight and blinded us. We were pushed back by the force of the rays and watched in wonder as Katia focused all of her positive energy onto her sister. Ambu seemed surprised but countered with her own dark powers, spewing black smoke and red laser beams directly at Katia. She was literally burning up with rage. Half the dome now glowed a brilliant white and the other half was an ominous red as the two sisters continued to battle it out in the middle. The walls of the dome became a reflection of their minds - Katia filled the room with happy memories whilst Ambu continued to show scenes of misery.

Around us, the golden dome trembled and we realised that whilst Ambu and Katia battled here, the Mermaids that followed Ambu were still directing their laser beams into the sky - the situation outside was clearly getting worse.

"LOLA, contact Banjo. I'm going to try and stop some of those rays," shouted Mr. Holt, as he dashed off to tackle a Mermaid to the ocean floor.

"Banjo, what are you seeing?" I closed my eyes and focused on reaching Banjo, hoping not to hear the worst.

"The waves are huge LOLA, and Main Beach is completely flooded. We've got protective shields up all across the coast, but I don't know how much longer we can hold it off," replied Banjo frantically. I could hear the panic in his voice.

"Tell everyone to hold their ground. We're doing all we can here, but it's a battle between Katia and Ambu. Right now, they are too evenly matched, so it's too hard to tell how this will end," I told him, genuinely starting to worry that we might not win this one.

I lost my connection to Banjo and turned around to see my friends fighting with the remaining Mermaids. Mr. Holt had managed to wrestle two of them to the ground and Allie was using the chains that had bound Katia to tie them up. Sparky was helping her, wrapping the Mermaids with his long tentacles and shocking them to keep them subdued. Paige and Eva were using their force fields to interrupt the laser beams shooting out of the dome and snap the Mermaids out of their trance.

It was chaos all around me.

I knew I should be doing something to help, but what?

I felt like I was stuck in a bad dream, and I couldn't move. I felt powerless to do anything.

And then suddenly, I knew exactly what to do. "Help them find a common bond," Reaya had told me. It seemed so obvious now, why hadn't I thought of it earlier?

I scanned through the memories in Katia's mind until I saw her clearly. She was beautiful, with deep emerald eyes and auburn curly hair that tumbled down her elegant back. Her tail flicked playfully as she looked lovingly at her two girls.

I filled the room with images of their Mother.

"Promise me one thing girls," her silky voice filled the gloom.

"Never forget who you are and why you're here..." both Ambu and Katia stopped abruptly and stared at the image in disbelief.

"You have both been given the most important job in the world and when your Father and I are gone, it will be up to you both to keep each other safe and protect the ocean." At the sound of their mother's voice Katia and Ambu were stopped dead in their tracks. They looked around and saw themselves as young girls staring back at their mother in adoration.

"Yes Mother," their younger selves told her.

"Good girls. Remember together you are stronger; you are like two halves of one whole and you must love and respect each other always," she told them, taking their two hands and interlocking their fingers together to create an unbreakable bond that she bound tightly with golden rope.

"Don't let me down now, I will always be with you," and with those words, the image faded and dissolved like vapour.

Ambu and Katia stood transfixed, staring at the empty space that their Mother had occupied just moments before.

I held my breath. All the fighting around them stopped and everyone stood completely still, waiting to see what would happen next.

Without warning, Ambu collapsed onto the floor sobbing. "Mother, Mother come back, come back," she wailed, banging her hands on the seabed.

Katia bent down and wrapped her arms around her sister. I could see waves of silver light shining from her body as she bathed her sister in love and compassion. Ambu seemed to extinguish on the floor like a flame snuffed out.

"There is another way Ambu, we can keep our promise to Mother," whispered Katia urgently.

"But the humans... they are killing everything! You've seen what will happen if we don't stop them," cried Ambu, who I could feel was genuinely afraid for the future and of the damage that humans were doing to the planet.

"Those visions I showed you, I didn't make those up you know... they are real! It wasn't me killing those innocent creatures, I'm not the one to blame here!" she said.

"I know that sister and I do agree that something needs to change. Humans have caused terrible harm to our planet, and it will taker a lot to reverse the damage but I truly believe that they are not evil by nature. There are many good humans that are fighting for the future of the planet. I believe that if we work together, we can fix things. It will take a lot of hard work, but if we combine our forces I know we can do this!" Katia promised her.

"Imagine that - you and I will be together again. It's what Mother and Father always wanted, for us to rule together!"

"But who will work with me now, everyone thinks I'm evil," said Ambu. "Admit it, they all think I'm some kind of monster. They call me the Ocean Monster. I'm a scary story that they tell their kids."

"No one knows that's you, they'll believe what I tell them. I'll introduce you as my long lost sister, who helped us defeat the Ocean Monster. You'll go down in history as the Mermaid who battled the ferocious Ocean Monster and won! Together, we can find a way to clean the ocean and protect future generations from disease and death. We can make the ocean a paradise once more like it was when we were kids, I promise you." Katia held out her hand to her sister. Ambu took it gingerly and then stood up to face her. After a few tense moments, they hugged each other and interlocked their fingers, recreating the bond their Mother had created all those years ago.

Whatever rage had consumed Ambu, it was now gone.

Standing before us now were two sisters, different in so many ways, yet united in their love for their Mother and the promise they made to her all those years ago.

It just goes to show you the power of a Mother's love.

I looked around at my friends, who were sighing with relief.

An awkward silence filled the room as the two sides reconciled. Just moments ago, we'd been in battle and now we had to find a way to work together. Reluctantly Paige, Eva and Allie turned their attention to the mermaids in chains and untied them.

I focused my attention on reaching Banjo - I had to let him know the good news.

"Banjo, can you hear me?"

"Oh LOLA, thank goodness, I thought the worst had happened. Are you all okay, and do you have Katia?" he asked frantically.

"Calm down Banjo, it's all going to be fine. Yes, we have Katia, and I'll explain everything when I see you. We're heading back to you now," I said.

"Oh that IS good news, everyone will be so pleased to see you. It's quite a mess here I'm afraid, but we've got a surprise for you. You wait until you see who turned up to help us," said Banjo mysteriously.

"Okay roger that, we're on our way," I told him, wondering who on earth he could possibly be talking about.

We left the Mermaid City together as one unified group. Katia convinced Ambu to make a fresh start, somewhere closer to shore so that they could get to know each other once again and the other mermaids seemed happy to follow her.

If you'd have asked me earlier if I really thought that a reunion was possible – that I'd be watching Ambu and Katia clutching hands like long lost sisters? Well, I'd have laughed at you! But it was happening right in front of my eyes, so it seems that love really does trump hate.

As we got closer to the shore, I could see the damage. Banjo had not exaggerated.

The tides had receded now, but the damage was widespread. The surf club and the human houses nearby were completely destroyed, and all that remained were the foundations and the debris that was strewn across the beach. Our caves were nowhere to be seen either. The floods had completely eroded the left side of the beach and formed a huge sandbank where we had once lived. The beach was covered by all manner of rubbish for as far as the eye could see. Fallen trees were strewn amongst broken boats and mountains of plastic that had been washed up by the waves. The sand was also home to hundreds of injured or dead animals, birds and sea creatures that had been washed up on the beach and needed urgent attention. The Water Fairies were doing all they could to tend to the sick and we rushed back to lend a helping hand.

"Who are all those little people over there?" cried Allie.

I looked to see who she was pointing at and sure enough over towards the lighthouse, I could see a long stream of little people moving down the beach. They were too small to be human, but they were too big to be fairies. How strange!

"There must be at least a hundred of them," said Allie.

"Ah," said Mr. Holt, smiling to himself. "I see now what Reaya was up to when she told you that she had an errand to run - she must have gone to get the Brownies and bring them here to help with the cleanup!" he said laughing.

"What do you mean? Do you know who they are?" I asked him.

"Yes, if I'm not mistaken they are the infamous Brownies. I have been following their antics quite closely. They are another type of magical creature that just loves to clean - they LIVE for it. Until very recently, they lived quietly in the kitchens of humans, never saying boo to a goose and only venturing out at night to do the cleaning. Then something happened, we're not sure what it was, but they left the humans and started causing

130

trouble all over the country – it was quite the scandal!" he replied.

"Cool, I've heard about Brownies before, I can't wait to meet them," I told him, squinting to get a better look at the little Brownies - who were short and squat and about ten inches tall. They all looked quite alike with their curly red hair, bobble noses, ruddy cheeks and no-nonsense manner. I'm not quite sure what they were wearing, but it looked like some kind of uniform. They had on what can only be described as knickerbockers, all frilly and fussy, but cut off into shorts. They also wore funky headbands in flowery material and little crop tops that showed off their round peachy bellies. They were quite adorable.

"I told Reaya about them the last time I saw her; she must have brought them here to help with the cleanup!" he said chuckling.

"Well they certainly came at the right time, that's for sure. I'd love to know their story," I told him.

"There's plenty of time for that LOLA, it's a long story and probably one best told by the Brownies themselves," answered Mr. Holt.

As intrigued as I was, I had to agree. I was grateful for their arrival, and the timing was perfect. I imagined that I'd learn their story all in good time. Besides I didn't want to interrupt their cleaning, after all they were famous for it!!

When we finally got back to Main Beach, everyone was so hard at work cleaning up that they didn't notice us arrive.

Banjo was the first to spot us.

"LOLA, Katia you're here… everyone, they're here, they're here!!" he buzzed excitedly around us, zipping up and down like a mad bee desperate to get everyone's attention.

Slowly, hundreds of tired faces turned to see us and lit up instantly. Katia was a welcome sight to her loyal army of Water Fairies, and they all flocked to her and exclaimed how happy they were to see her back safe and sound.

Ambu hung back nervously (after all she was the cause of all this mess!), but Katia pulled her to the front and hugged her close. She introduced Ambu to the Water Fairies as her long lost sister and they accepted her word without question.

I looked around, trying to find Jet and Eddie. I spotted them further up the beach and made my way over to them. They were surrounded by the infamous Brownies, who were all carrying big sacks on their backs and filling them with trash.

"LOLA, you decided to come and lend a hand finally, did you?" asked Jet cheekily.

"Yeah, there was not much going on where I was, so I thought I'd better come and help you out!" I replied, laughing at his joke.

"Nice, well as you can see, we've got a bit of cleaning up to do," he added, pointing to the general mess that lay in every single direction.

"I can see you've found some helpers though," I said, looking at the Brownies scurrying around the beach, cleaning up like they were against the clock.

"I tell you what, I have no idea where these lot came from, but I'm mighty glad they did. They are demons at cleaning, we can't keep up with them. Can we Eddie?" answered Jet.

"You're not wrong, I could do with one or two of these Brownies at my house, well what's left of my house that is..." said Eddie, faltering off as he realised that he probably didn't have much of a home to go back to.

"We can start again, we've been here before haven't we LOLA?" and Jet gave me a knowing look.

"Yes, it seems to be a trend! Let's try and keep the next home for a bit longer, shall we?" I said, slightly amused at the ridiculousness of the situation.

We worked together into the dead of night, side-by-side with the Water Fairies, Mermaids and Brownies working as one. As the sun rose, Katia whistled to get our attention. We all stopped what we were doing and stared in wonder as a huge convoy of humans made their way onto the beach - the crowd was full of both the young and the old, some carrying signs, some playing music, but all of them were there to cleanup the beach. The leaders at the front of the convoy were shouting through a loudspeaker

"SAVE OUR OCEANS!!" shouted one, and the crowd chanted along.

"SAY NO TO PLASTIC!!" shouted the others, and again the crowd chanted along.

Katia glimmered the beach to ensure that the humans would not see us already busy at work. They had arrived to help and we had no intention of stopping them or distracting them. Between us, we could make a REAL difference. If we worked by night and they worked by day, eventually we could rid the oceans and the beaches of everything that didn't belong there.

There was still hope and there's nothing we fairies like more than hope.

THE END

Actually,
the best
gift you
could have
given her
was a lifetime
of adventures...

~ Lewis Carroll
Alice in Wonderland

ACKNOWLEDGEMENTS

I've heard other authors say that the second novel is a lot harder to write than the first - that's certainly been my experience. A laptop meltdown, lost manuscript, loss of faith and many other things occurred during the writing of this my second novel and I am extremely grateful to everyone who helped me navigate through the ups and downs.

First and foremost to my ah-mazing husband, you know why!

Secondly thanks again to my top-notch illustrator Craig Phillips who brought Lola and her friends beautifully to life once again.

Thanks to my first readers and proudest supporters, Mum, my bro Lee and best friend Chloe for your most excellent advice and suggestions, you seem to know exactly what I'm struggling with and have the right advice at exactly the right time.

Thanks to my editor Aarti for understanding exactly what the story needed and challenging me to do better, I'm lucky to have crossed paths with you.

To all my friends, for just being awesome humans and encouraging me on my new path, but special mentions must go out Chloe, Camilla, Kate and my brother for making the most noise out there on the 'interwebs' – love and respect.

Lastly but definitely not least thanks to every single girl and boy that enjoyed reading Lola and took the time to tell me so. It means everything to me when I hear from a young reader so please keep telling me what you think and I'm open to suggestions on where you'd like Lola to go next!

ABOUT THE AUTHOR

Jade Harley worked in the media industry for twenty years, as Managing Editor of a variety of music, lifestyle and fashion titles and Managing Director of a digital media business. She now splits her time between writing novels and consulting to businesses and not for profit organisations that she's passionate about.

The Adventures of Lola and the Ocean Monster is the second novel by Harley in a planned series following Lola's adventures. A fierce conservationist, vegan and lover of nature and animals, Harley hopes to inspire young girls to dream big, explore, and protect the environment.

Harley was born in Britain and now lives in Australia.

For more information visit the website www.theadventuresoflola.com

Made in the USA
Columbia, SC
07 October 2021